TO TELL MY PEOPLE

Books for Young People
by Madeleine Polland

BRITAIN

LANDING PLACE OF CAESAR

×
↑
LUMNA'S
LAKE

GAUL

SPAIN

MIDDLE   SEA

TO TELL MY PEOPLE

by Madeleine Polland

illustrated by Richard M. Powers

HOLT, RINEHART AND WINSTON
New York   Chicago   San Francisco

TO TELL MY PEOPLE

Chapter One

CIVILIZATION had not reached down into the green marshy swamps between the two ridges of downland. Progress marched busily along the uplands, forming thriving settlements and camps where soil was light and easy to plough, but the low weald was left alone; to the dark tangling forest and the silence of the brown reeking marshlands, with here and there a small ancient village crouching on some lonely lake with small fields about its edge and low rank pastures for the grazing cattle.

On such a settlement lived Lumna, her island village huddled over the reed-grown water behind its woven palisades, though two generations could tell no story of when an enemy had last approached the barren and forgotten place. On all sides the forest rolled down dark and thick, closing so close that through many daylight hours its shadow filled the lake; only the high times of the sun warmed the water and the few fields around it to a close and steamy heat.

Lumna hated it, hated the rolling forest rearing its high wall all around the village, closing out all the the world that lay beyond it. She alone of all the people in the village cherished like a secret treasure in her mind the knowledge that such a world was there. Twelve times, although she could not count, she had seen the sun rise to its highest in the warm middle months of the year. Seven times she had watched it with her father's mother, and she alone in the tribe seemed to remember the tales the old woman had told of this high day in her own distant part of the land far toward the sunset. The old woman had talked to her—almost as though she had been forbidden to talk to anyone else—secret tales whispered under the close warmth of piled skins on winter nights, or by the cool lakeside in the sun while others worked, she too old and the little girl too young to have to join them.

Lumna had listened, her deep-set eyes growing blue and dark with wonder, listened to tales of some part of her land where the sunrise swept like lake water over a great plain stretching green and rich as far as eye could see; and on the high day of summer, man trapped the sunrise in a mighty ring of stones, measuring the falling of their shadows, and learning from them the past and the future and all the secrets of the earth. Death was there and blood and terror, and fearful ceremonies, some of which the old woman would whisper in secret watchful horror, and some of which she would not tell at all.

She told her too how the people of her time had lived out in the open on the hills, in wide-spaced huts that took the sun above the high banks of their defenses. Told her how they knew of the lands beyond their walls from men who traveled to the far mountains for the quarrying of the great stones. Lumna knew nothing. Beyond the green wall of the forest stretched a world unknown to her, spoken of only by the old woman, now long dead. Now in her thirteenth year she brooded over all these half-forgotten things, and the long green days tore her with restlessness and resentment. She longed to break through the forest wall to see this world for herself.

But she might as well have been sealed in by the vast gray stones of the old woman's tales. Her tribe knew of no world beyond their lake nor did they care, but she had lately dreamed incessantly of wide spaces of empty grass, of wind and vast clear skies and ways of life half understood, which this small buried tribe had never thought of.

"Lumna! Always idling with an empty head! How much is done since I left you?"

The girl started and looked guiltily across through the smoke hazing the low-roofed hut. All light was blocked by the square bulk of her mother's body in the door, and her harsh, angry voice blocked out abruptly all foolish dreams of wide skies and a richer world beyond the forest. Vaguely the girl looked down at a pile of fresh-cut rushes lying by her hand, and at the strong osiers ready to plait with them into a new basket for the fish. She had barely begun, the rushes fallen from her idle fingers while her eyes dreamed on the dying fire.

The mother struggled in through the low doorway, banging the doorposts with the crude yoke that held two brimming tubs of milk, slopping it over to sour there on the earthen floor; another smell to add to all that clung already to the smoke-filled air. As though her angry voice gave them a signal, the younger children playing in the dusty shadows set up dismal howling, missing her only now that she was back. Against them she raised her voice to go on scolding the girl beside the fire.

"Useless! Always with your feet in the ashes or gone rambling away there up on the hill with eyes as empty as the lake water or the heads of the dead that live there, and no hands to offer for the household work. Who is Lumna that the rest of the family must keep her from all toil? Lumna the lazy for whom all others must work!"

Her voice was sharpened by the edges of all her own anxieties, hard and bitter with the monstrous toil of wresting a living from this dry patch in the middle of the endless swamp, and from the efforts of the small tribe against the strength of savage nature that could overwhelm them all in one careless season, as though man had never been. No pair of hands could be spared from the ceaseless struggle.

Lumna looked up at her as she moved from the doorway, letting sun fall in again to light the smoky dwelling. She was barely as tall as the girl herself, barefoot and rough-haired, in a coarse brown woolen garment, woven as the old woman had taught them all to weave, on the crude loom in the corner of the hut. When the winter came, she would join a couple of wolfskins and add them to her tunic against the damp, creeping cold. Her hair fell tangled down into her eyes, deep set like Lumna's in a high-boned face, brown and stained with all the work and summers of her life.

"She is no more," Lumna said to herself blindly, barely knowing the cause of her own sudden fury, hating her ugliness as the mother turned to aim a sharp kick at one of the howling children. "No more almost than the cattle in the pastures. There must be more than this for people, must be more, more. The old woman told me that there was!"

Suddenly, the harsh, scolding voice and the wailing children grew more than she could stand. On the tripod set above the fire, water boiled over to add to the noise with hiss and sputter in the ashes, and against her mother's furious shriek and the clouds of steam rising with the turf reek, Lumna's anger boiled in the same instant. With a bare, angry foot she kicked the pile of rushes into the hissing edges of the fire, stilling her mother's voice into an instant of appalled silence. In their narrow scheme of life there was no room for waste. Pushing aside the yowling babies, she stampeded through the open door, turning to shout back at her mother as she went.

"Make your own baskets," she shouted. "Set your own cheese! Lumna do this, Lumna do that. I am tired

of it! There are other things," she added blindly, breaking now to the edge of tears. "Other things! The old
woman said so!"

The mother made no attempt to follow her, standing
only in silence to watch her go. Once outside the hut,
Lumna slowed to a walk, conscious of the eyes that
watched her through the doorways and the ears that
listened to every smallest thing that passed. She would
be gossip for them around their evening fires; already
she was talked about in the tribe as proud Lumna who
always walked alone.

Tossing back her long, light brown hair, and lifting
her small narrow head to the sun, she marched through
the beaten earthen paths of the village, and out along
the crumbling causeway to the water's edge, still seething with the angry certainty born of her memories of the
old woman that there must be more to the world than
howling children and a shouting mother in a dirty hut
—and she could find it. But certainty faded with the
silence as she poled the small wicker boat across the
glass-green water to the meadows. The lake was hazed
with midges in the windless afternoon and marked with
the small sudden circles of jumping fish.

By the time she had reached the wooden jetty on the
lakeside, she had calmed, and knew dumbly and de-
spairingly what she had always known, that all she
could do about such things was dream of them. For
her, all her life, there would be no more than the secret
lake and the crowded huts, smoke and darkness and
cold and squabbling children, and in the end a hut of

her own with some boy of the tribe of her father's choosing. Even if there *was* a world beyond, how could she, a girl, go out to seek it through the forest? But at least there was one place she could go awhile before she had to turn back and face her mother and the inevitable beating for idleness and waste, one place where there was peace to imagine the old woman's wide skies and the world that lay beyond her tribe—the world she would never find.

Carefully she skirted the pastures, where she could see her father and her brothers among the cattle. Better keep out of their way lest they find some task for her to do. She took the pathway of the dead, for only those for burial went the winding way in their sad processions up this hill, to the place where her tribe and tribes before it had brought their dead, right back into the legendary days of the Ancient People. Once she had been found there by a chanting funeral, and her mother had stared at her with horror and not a little fear.

"Why do you go there?"

Lumna had stared back defiantly, and then around the crowded, noisy hut.

"It is quiet."

"Quiet!" The mother made a gesture of one who would avert a curse. "The dead are always quiet. See you do not become one of them. Where they are is no place for the living!"

On the lower slopes above the lake, the track was quite plain and wide, used by the tribe regularly, branched here and there with clear hunting paths. But gradually, as the land rose more sharply, the track got overgrown, and Lumna had to push her way through the young spreading suckers of briars and bushes, thrusting aside small springy saplings, following a path up to the sun that belonged almost to her alone.

There was another place up here as well as the burial ground, belonging to the tribe. The elders said it had been here since the days of the Ancient People, who had lived in it; but now it was a place of fear and superstition, avoided by the people except for Lumna's father, who saw it clearly as a strong and secret hideout in the face of enemies, and came occasionally with his sons to be sure the trap door was cleared of bush, the shafts open for air, and the whole place fit for habitation if it was needed. But the longest days passed, and the shortest, in the cycles of the sun, year after year, and no enemy troubled the forgotten village on the lake. Only Lumna struggled frequently up the steep hillside until the forest thinned to sapling trees and bushes and the sharp painful drag of blackberry thorns. Finally, with the sun now hot on her thick hair, the first round crest of the hill rose above the forest trees, capped with short fine turf, scattered with fragrant herbs and heady with the sun-drenched perfume of the yellow whins. All was silent in the dead heat save for the high shrilling of the larks and the crickets clicking in the short grass.

Awhile she rested, out of sight of the lake and the cluster of huts like beehives on the island in its center, letting the thought of dirt and darkness and the peering tribe slide from her mind as though blown by the wind ruffling the tree tops far below her. She stared away at the opposite hills, rising above their own piled forests to a bare ridge against the distant sky, hills looking exactly as her own yet so far away that surely they must belong to the other world whose vision haunted her, far hills lying certainly under a wide sky. For Lumna, even here, high above her world, forest rose behind her to the top ridge of the hills, and for her, the wide skies lay forever in the distance and in the stories of the old one. Suddenly she blinked sharply, throwing up her hands to shield her eyes, not understanding why she did so. Some brief startling light had seemed to flash from the other hills, as when the sun struck sudden blaze from lake water ruffled by the wind, no sooner come than gone. But from here she could not see the lake, buried in its ring of forest. Her hands dropped and she stared puzzled over the long sweep of valley, slumbering in the sun now well past noon; nothing stirring in the whole great rolling stretch of trees. As she turned away, the light flashed out again, flashing and flashing yet again, now long, now short, now long, and even though she screwed her eyes and closed them, the white flashes seared on, scarlet across her tight shut lids. Long and short and long and long.

Suddenly she was desperately afraid. Sun she knew, on land and water in all its phases, and the red and yellow lights of fire, blazing to colors with soaked timbers from the lake. But this white flashing held for her a cold, senseless terror, coming suddenly like a silent enemy from some strange world she did not know. She forgot all her dreams of knowing strange worlds, of learning anything beyond her tribe, and scrambled blindly to her feet. But before she could run, the light vanished and the far hills lay untroubled, taunting her in sun-soaked quiet to believe what she had seen. She stood there shivering foolishly in the heat, shaking under the threat of this nameless, formless harm, no sound about her but the larks singing and a small cool wind now whispering gently through the grass. Nothing to see across the valley; nothing to trouble her on her own quiet hill.

Now she did not run, but turned and moved slowly toward her private place of peace and silence to calm herself and try to understand it, for she could never tell of it, and face the jeering faces of her tribe.

"Lumna again," they would say. "Trying always to be different and to know things that are not for others."

The light blazed again, blinding against the dark background of the trees, and in panic fear of some un-heard-of harm, she leaped for safety, her eyes behind her on the brilliant flashes even as her fingers groped for the familiar bronze ring. It was set in a great stone slab, sunk into the hill itself, too heavy for the hands of any man, but so constructed by the Ancient People that just a gentle pull from Lumna moved it around in its holding grooves. Inside was the long, sloping passage leading down gently into the abandoned habitation.

She stood there some time, feeling the safety of the heavy stone between her and the bright outside world filled so suddenly with senseless terror. Leaning her back on the cool wall and pushing her hair from her eyes, fear seeped away in all that was familiar as she breathed in the soft, dank smell of the moss along the passage pavings, and the small rocky plants forcing themselves out along the crevices of the walls. The big chamber at the end of the curving passage she knew to be warm and dry. Stones were too closely laid even for the thrusting roots of grass, and the sun struck like a spear shaft down through the opening in the great slabs of the ceiling, green and shifting on the pale floor from the shadows of the trees blowing out above it on the hill. Making smoke only in the hours of darkness, a tribe could live here safe in hiding through the ravaging of its land, moving back afterward to rebuild some burnt and shattered village.

In the big chamber in the green shifting sunlight, with fingers of shadow creeping on the pale stone walls, there was always peace, peace to rest and listen to the silence, and the larks rising on the hill outside. Here there were whispers of this wider world she longed to know about. Here in this gray silence was a hint of the strange tales of the enormous stones, and of a land where men did more than sleep and wake and quarrel and search for food and sleep again in the endless silent reflections of their lonely lake, where men did more than tend a few stringy cows and fish the sleepy water. But what?

Lumna shook herself, clearing the dreams that always threatened to swamp her here. Useless to pretend she did not have to go back, that she was not a silent and brooding lake dweller like all the others. She thrust her fingers tiredly through her long brown hair, not coarse and tangled like her mother's, but straight and heavy, for she had learned to keep the roughness from it with a brush of long, stiff thorns, and learned also that it felt softer and sweeter if she dipped it in the water of the lake in the mornings. She knew her face was narrow and her forehead low under the thick hair, but that her eyes were large and beautiful and deep-shadowed, for she had found without understanding it that, when the sun was behind her and the water still, the lake held a drowned figure that could be only hers. It moved when she moved, and smiled to her smile, vanishing in a thousand shattered fragments with the movement of the wind.

Quietly and aimlessly, relaxing in known peace and safety, putting off the moment when she must go out and face not only her angry mother, but also the strange terror flashing on the hills, she drifted down the long passage, fingers trailing idly along the cool rough stone. Absently, her eyes heedless, she turned at the end into the sun-warmed light of the big chamber.

When she thought about this moment afterward, she knew that it was only because she was so small that no spear had instantly split her through her chest. The group at the far end of the chamber had been expecting a man, or men, and from their faces it was clear they had waited only for an enemy, spears ready at their shoulders. At first she did not know what they might be, so strange were they to her astonished eyes. They stood close together in a small ring at the far end of the big round chamber, all their spears pointing outward, clearly listening in taut silence to the scuffing of her feet and her trailing hands as she had drifted down along the passage. The first thing she really noticed was relief and some amusement on their brown faces as she came out of the passage and stared back at them, as astonished as they. One only she recognized as a person of her own kind, a boy a little older than herself, with fairer hair and a long knobbly face, spear as ready as the rest to leave his shoulder.

Grins spread over all the round brown faces, slightly sheepish, and spears trailed to the ground, until a man with red stripes about his sleeve ends and a cloak of aching scarlet rolled above his shoulders spoke to them sharply in some smooth liquid tongue; then the spears came up again in chilly threat. He had not smiled at her nor had he seemed relieved.

Red Stripe spoke again to the boy, who looked at him and moved toward Lumna. She did not understand the words that Red Stripe spoke, but she knew the tongue of spears in any land, and knew also suddenly that life was life, even on her lonely island, and death was cold and frightening and forever, without the sun and the cool friendly rock and all the shifting shadows. But at last in front of her, the boy dropped his spearpoint, and death slipped back again to be a thing for others. He spoke to her, not in the tongue of her tribe, but in words so much the same that she could manage

to follow him, understanding even some of his actual words.

"No one will harm you, girl. My centurion wants to know if you are alone." This she did not understand. "Are there more with you?" he asked slowly.

Dumbly she shook her head, still too close to fear of death to speak, to understand that she could try to answer, that some of the same words belonged to both of them. Her blue eyes only gained the courage to flicker upward, and watch them as they spoke together. They were all taller than her father, taller than any of her tribe, with round, dark-skinned faces and close-

fitting clothes, cut cunningly into the same shape as their bodies. Leather, she thought, still with most of her mind on the bristling spears, seeing it all like some fantastic vision of her sleep. Metal glinted everywhere on the leather, in studs and strings of small bright rings, and their heads were covered in round caps of it, flaps of leather hanging down over their ears. Her bewildered eyes fell to their feet, finding them wearing shoes cut to fit them like their clothes, some with long leather casings laced up to their knees.

Plastered against her wall as though it were her only safety, she watched three of them come past her on a word from Red Stripe, who clearly searched the long passage to see if what she had said was true. They walked like ordinary men, even in the high stiff leather, with soles that rang upon the stones. She heard the soft familiar groan of the moving stone as they looked out over the hillside before coming back again to report to Red Stripe, who spoke in turn to one who was taller than the rest, and thinner, his rolled cloak a warm, splendid color, glowing in the green filtered light, not blue, not red, but perhaps if you could mix them both? He too had stripes on his brown sleeves of the same rich color as his cloak.

Spears were grounded and some of the creatures were laughing, looking at each other and at her. One of them took off his metal cap and underneath it his head was as round as his face, all his hair close-cropped like the chalkland turf of the hill outside. From the edge of the group the boy watched her steadily and curiously, and

16

his fair face was not unfriendly, but he did not speak again. Away to one side talked the two men with stripes on their brown sleeves.

The thin one spoke; the tribune. "Laughable, my good Flavius," he said with a faint smile, "to have the whole party quivering like reeds for one small girl, but I was not ready to have all my work undone by some tribe thundering in to get their corn."

Flavius, the centurion, looked around him.

"No corn here, sir. But good storage. No tribe either that we can see, but she must come from somewhere. Question her, sir?"

"Not in your ways, Flavius. She is only a child."

Routine discipline stiffened Flavius' face.

"Child must know if she lives in a village, and where it is."

"I am more concerned at this stage that the village does not know where we are."

"Better kill then, my lord Durus, and no more questions." A barely perceptible twitch of his jaw belied the cold practical words, but the thin young man with the purple cloak frowned again.

"Always so abrupt, my Flavius," he said with distaste. "Bring me the child, and my boy Cassilus. Two years in Belgian swamps have taught me enough perhaps to ask my own questions. She seemed to understand the boy as long as he spoke slowly."

Stiffly, and officially disapproving, Flavius marched a step away from his superior before opening his mouth and bawling for the boy, and every soldier raised a startled head to the echoes battering from stone to stone around the curving roof.

Lumna crept forward at the boy's bidding, stunned with terror at the rumbling echoes which her own gentle murmurings had never raised, linking them in fear with the blazing light outside and the sudden coming of these beings from some other world. Some other world. Dimly her mind groped back through clouds of fear to the talking of the old woman, who spoke of beings greater than the men of earth, beings for whom these dreadful mysteries were held in the great ring of stones, beings who demanded death and blood without end, that they might not loose their anger on the people. What had they been called? The lake tribe had never troubled with these things. They had slipped down out of their minds in their narrowing world that reckoned only on the filling of their stomachs. Gods! Whispered remembered words of sacrifice on vast flat stones at the reckoned moments of the sun, of safety and victory in battle, of strength and fine weather and good crops and many children, all bought from these far beings with offerings of poured blood and ravaged dead, crowded her frightened mind.

"Girl!"

She tore her eyes from the patient face of the young tribune, Durus, who had eased his helmet from his hot head, tore her eyes from the neat, close curls clustering around his head above his clean shaven face, from the fine soft stuff of his tunic and the splendid color of his cloak. Was this a being to demand such endless death?

Almost blindly she stared at the boy who had shouted at her, troubling again the faint echoes of the roof. Flavius stood by, his square face immobile and disapproving.

"Three times I ask," the boy cried, banging his words out one by one. "Tell my lord here who you are and where you live and how many in your tribe, and what food and weapons they may have!"

In a while, the young man questioned her also, in the halting words he had picked up in two long, cold years among the newly conquered tribes of Belgium, which were like her own, and yet were not. Slowly he picked from her all he wanted to know, speaking gently to her blank and fearful face. Then he turned to Flavius and spoke in the smooth tongue she did not understand.

Flavius grunted sourly.

"Lake people," he said with contempt. "Savages. No use to us or to themselves. We had best, sir, frighten her to still her tongue and go. We've been here long enough. Her tribe will be no trouble even if we cross them. Savages," he said again, and spat contemptuously and expertly between the pavings of the floor.

While they talked, Lumna, her eyes ranging furiously from one to the other, had been gathering her courage. Fear was fading a little with the grounded spears, and taking its place was a desperate desire to know even if in the end the result was truly blood and sacrifice, and hers the death they would demand. She fumbled for the words, not knowing how to call this handsome figure with the purple cloak and the high leather boots, whose sober eyes watched her above his thin curved nose. "Chief," she said suddenly and desperately in the end, as the people of her tribe would call her father. She could not be bothered with the boy, who was ordinary, like herself. She must speak directly to this being, and be sure of the answer to her question. The gray eyes focused on her with surprise, and Flavius bristled, to be stilled with a gesture from a hand more long-fingered and clean than any Lumna knew. Waiting eyebrows told her to go on speaking.

"Chief," she began again, and then could find no words to be less than totally abrupt. "Are you gods?" she blurted out.

From the corners of her eyes she caught the expression of delighted hilarity on the boy's face, and the grin he shot at the man, but Durus Velanius himself did not smile. Gravely he looked back at her.

"What do you know of gods?" he asked her, and stumbling, she told him as best she could of the old woman's tales—the great rings of stones and the cycles of the sun, and the beings who asked for endless blood— and the boy no longer smiled but stared at her in tolerant contempt. Only the tribune continued to watch her in grave quiet, and waited a moment of silence after she had faltered to a stop.

"Yes," he said then, definitely and emphatically. "We are gods."

For some reason the boy gasped at his side, and stared with open mouth, gaining from the man an exasperated glance.

"We are gods," he said then again to the girl. "And your grandmother has told you of the terrible fates we demand for those who betray us. Fearful death for those who speak of us when they have seen us. Tell no one what you have seen today, and you are safe. Death if you speak." Barely she understood him, but she understood enough.

Through the shaking of belief and fear, she could not but notice the changing expression of the boy, grinning at her now as though she was one of the simple ones of the tribe who grew in stature like men and women, but never left their childhood, paddling and chattering around the edges of the lake. But her eyes were held by the severe gray ones of the man, and her mind by the flashing lights and the thunder of the roof above her head. Looking at his close-cropped hair and rounded head and fine brown skin, she knew him certainly as never of her world, nor of the world of common men, and she did not doubt his word. Gods they were, and he the greatest, and death was hers if she should speak of them. What matter that she must be secret. The tribe would hold their ribs with laughter if she went down to them with this. Lumna again, dreaming dreams, and knowing more than anybody else.

"I will not tell," she said then reverently, and the god inclined his head. He spoke then to Flavius, who glanced at the girl and gave a short bark of laughter, his eyes showing he would much sooner settle any matter with the short edge of his sword than with this long exchange of muddled words.

"I hope you do right, sir," was all he said, and the tribune lost his godlike calm.

"Great Caesar wants Britain, Flavius," he said irritably. "But I do not demand the blood of every little savage that I come across. Get the men moving. Fear of the gods will close her mouth as certainly as death."

They went without another glance at her, where she stood again flattened against the wall to watch them go, the red cloak leading, all the brown ones in between, and the purple bringing up the rear. They were all out of sight, and only their footsteps were still dull on the damp stones, when suddenly the boy came running back. He stood a moment in front of her, his close face growing in the instant as oddly familiar as if she had known it all her life, with its long, narrow cheeks, and heavy-lidded eyes looking her up and down, unwilling to believe that anyone could be so simple.

"They are not gods, girl," he said contemptuously. "They are *Romans*! Romans! But do not tell of that either, or you will just as surely die. Gods," he snorted, and did not wait for her to answer.

She stared after him, unmoving, as he ran off again.

Romans? Or gods? One was the same as the other, not of this her ordinary world, except that she had heard of gods, but never of Romans. Before she gathered her frightened legs to take her along the passage, she looked up searchingly at the familiar roof, but silence lay across its curving stones, and when she came out onto the hill, the far trees were dark and undisturbed in the failing sun.

Chapter Two

SHE almost did not notice the inevitable beating from her furious mother when she got back to the dwelling, her mind absent on the remote beings who had vanished on the hill. Only when dark had fallen and the whole family gathered in the firelit gloom did she look around her and see her home with shaken loathing such as she had never known in all her discontent.

Fire smoke was acrid in her breathing, eddying through the low dwelling, mixing its dryness with the smells of cooking and soured milk and untended babies and the haunting leather tang of the piled skins around the walls where all the family slept. Dust rose from the beaten floor with every moving foot, and she saw her father's brother, whom she hated, stumble on the floor where the leaking thatch had scoured a hole deep as a man's head. She watched her father's hand gripping a bone he tore to pieces with his teeth, short-fingered and broken at the nails, grained with the dirt of his working life. Beside him her mother, her tangled hair falling to her food, shapeless in her brown tunic, while a small child clutched and wailed at her other side. Lumna looked at her hands, and into her mind swam a picture of the clean, long-fingered hand that had silenced Red Stripe with a gesture. The girl looked down at her own hands and legs. A little better, since it was summer, and she could jump into the cold lake in the mornings.

But dirty, she thought, her mind again on the clean brown ones of the god. I had not known that we are dirty.

In the acrid glow of firelight, her eyes roamed her family: shapeless and unclean, barefoot or with crude coverings of skin tied like a bag about their ankles.

These gods, she brooded, know more things than we. They know how their clothes should be the same shape as their bodies, their shoes the same shape as their feet. What more do they know, and how do they know it? Where did gods live that they knew so much more than ordinary men? Why could her tribe not know these things too, and live no more in smoke and dirt and darkness? Her eyes grew wide with confused dreams of all she had seen today and all she had heard long ago from the old woman. What if these two worlds were one, existing here in her own land but far toward the sunset? Was she not young, and strong enough to make this journey, to find these things and bring them to her people? Her own joint drooped uneaten in her hand, grease patching unheeded on her tunic as she stared into the failing fire, scarlet wood graying and crumbling into ash. Suddenly, as if he had spoken, she felt her father's eyes on her for one long moment as though they were alone, without the crying children and the arguing uncles and the grumbling mother and the boys fighting in the corner of the hut. She blinked and looked at him again, bewildered by some feeling that he knew her thoughts. Her father, to whom she barely spoke? For the men and women of the tribe lived much apart, and fathers and daughters knew little of each other.

He turned away then, to his food, and it was as if some door closed that had stood for a moment open, and the dwelling pressed on her once more in all its noise and smells and darkness. Today had taught her caution, for her beaten back still smarted, and though she longed to run again as she had run that afternoon, she waited patiently now until the meal was done, and she got the task of getting water from the lake to clean the few wooden bowls and platters.

She lingered dangerously long over the dipping of the pails, but there was no answer to her questions in the dark starlit water shattering into drifting rings about her bucket, no answer from the crowded village at her back, warm and friendly as she turned from the causeway, firelight shining from its doors and shadows moving between the dwellings, smoke in pale columns rising to the dark skies above its roofs. No answer, nor dare she ask, for that was death for her.

Silent and withdrawn, she climbed between her own

pile of skins against the hot sleeping bodies of her smaller sisters, and sleep took her too, quickly. But her last thought was of the gods and the death they threatened. Was that where they came from? From beyond the secrets of death, from the place of the Ancient People?

In the early morning, she trailed a line in the lake, absently seeking the fish that jumped all around her, small, sudden-shining circles widening on the placid water; grateful to be doing something that would please her mother and yet leave her alone, out in the clear air and the silence. From the causeway her father hailed her, looking for the boat to cross the lake. She ferried the small skin craft over to him and he climbed in from the tumbled stones.

It would be usual for her not to speak, taking him in silence to the far shore, questioning nothing, but the strange moment of communion through the smoke the previous night gave her new courage, and her seething mind had desperate need to speak with someone. Yet she was still timorous, searching for the first words.

"Where are you going, Father?" she asked him, sweeping the smooth lake away behind her with her paddle, thinking him going no more than into the lake-side fields, as was usual.

From under his thick brown hair he looked at her in some surprise, but he answered kindly.

"Up the hill," he said, "to the place of the Ancient People." He showed her a small skin bag. "I take grease to put on the hinges of the stone, lest we ever need to use it in a hurry."

Now she stared at him, mouth fallen open, the paddle limp in her hands. What if the gods were there again? This time the spears might be thrown, seeing a man and not a child. How could she tell him, and death not take her?

"Something is wrong," he asked her then, "that we sit like swans in the middle of the lake?"

She had not known him ever to joke with her. Surprise and pleasure caught her with a warm sudden smile, and then a greater urgency that he must not go up the hill. There was something that she could tell him that the gods had not forbidden, that might frighten him as it had frightened her.

"In the noon of the last sun," she said, "I was up on the hill myself."

Now he looked at her again, with deep eyes, like her own, of great beauty under overhanging brows. Concern filled them, and warning, such as never filled her mother's.

"One day a wolf will get you, daughter, if you climb the hill alone. And the Ancient People may not like it. It is their place."

"Is it?" she wondered, as she had wondered the night before. Had she seen the Ancient People themselves from their place of the dead?

"I like it because it is lonely," was all she said. "And," she added thoughtfully, "I have never seen a wolf on that side of the forest. Maybe the dead keep them away. No, I saw something else, more frightening than any wolf."

They bumped gently to the bank of the lake, and without any words Lumna knew that she would walk with him up the hill. Nor did he protest as she tied the small boat to the mooring post, and made to follow him across the field. His silence gave her consent to speak and, crossing the familiar sunlit meadow, she told him as best she could of the bright dazzling light that had flashed and flashed in such strange terror on the distant hills. Almost running to look back up into his face, she waited for a fear to echo her own, to make him turn and say he would not go up the hill. But he plodded on, iron-tipped spear up-ended for a staff, shaking his head a little, not deeply interested. It was something beyond his world, and it was hard enough to live in that, without seeking for more outside it.

"There are many such things," he said, almost reluctantly in the end. "There is a place you must have seen from the hill, where smoke rises in a great column in the day, and the red glow of fire hangs over it at night."

Lumna nodded. Smoke was smoke and there was no fear in it. She did not add that nothing would bring her to climb up among the dead at night. The smoke was always there, like the forest trees, and it had not occurred to her to question it.

"It is something?" she asked when he did not go on. Perhaps, after all, the smoke was some part of the wider world; might it be some help in understanding about the gods?

"It is the place," her father said slowly, as if telling of

some unnecessary thing new to him, like having his daughter here beside him instead of one of his sons, who never spoke themselves and asked to be told nothing more than the plain rules of how to stay alive. "It is the place where men dig great lumps of certain soil out of the ground and place it in a huge fire. When it is hot it runs like water, so that they can beat it with their hammers into shapes, while red sparks fly out in rain. Then they plunge it into water so that the steam rises like mist on the lake, with a great hissing, and then the cooled earth is hard forever and cannot break. Thus my spear."

He touched the up-ended iron tip of his spear, and Lumna stared at him in amazement. Never had she heard so many words from him in her young life, and he had laid before her so clear a picture of the iron-making that it brought to her mind at once the tales of the old woman, who had made for her the same word pictures of her lost world.

"Father," she said in astonishment, and it was clear in her voice, "you are like the old woman."

His fine eyes slid around to her in a warm amusement she had not thought possible from his distant silence.

"Did you think, daughter, that you and the old woman were the only ones in the tribe with words to use?"

Lumna was blunt. "You have never used them."

She watched the light die from her father's face and was touched with some sudden grief she did not understand.

"No," he said then. "There is not much need for words about the lake."

She was so astonished that she said no more for a long time, but followed him in silence up the narrow trail. They heard a wild boar snorting in the thickets and left him carefully in peace. Small creatures scurried from their coming, and the crickets were loud in the long grass. As the sun grew higher, the trees were filled with the soft endless brooding of the doves.

They came into a small clearing close to the open top of the hill, and she came up beside him, bursting to put into words all that had been filling her mind as she followed him.

"Father, did you listen to the old woman?"

"All my youth," he answered.

"And did you believe her?"

"Why not?"

"Then you did not care?"

"Care about what?"

"The world beyond the island and the lake. Did you not want to go and find out the things she said, and see them for yourself?" She looked up toward where the clear round top of the hill showed between the thinning trees, and shivered. "I am afraid, very much afraid of the flashing lights, but I would like to find them and know them for what they are, like you know about the smoke." To herself she added, And I would like to know about the gods, but this I dare not ask.

"I had to know about the smoke," he said. "I needed iron."

"Who told you?" she asked curiously.

He shrugged. "I do not know. You learn what you have to know."

"And no more?"

He stopped and looked at her a long time before he spoke, and now the deep-set eyes under the thick brows were sad.

"You are," he said, "the old woman come back to us. Always she told me not to stay in the swamp, but to take my tribe and go toward the sunset on the rising land. There, she said, was the world."

He was so long silent that she could not help but prompt him, to rouse these eyes staring at her as if they did not see her.

"You did not go?"

His eyes focused on her again, and hopelessly he shrugged.

"The tribe would not go. They would have killed me if I tried to leave them, and I was their chief. They were my task and they were my people. Your people too, to whom you belong." He made a dismissing gesture with his hands. "Now I do not mind. I have not minded for more suns than I can remember, nor thought of these things until you came to plague me." He turned again up the slope of the hill.

There was a small pool in the open clearing, and Lumna stood awhile before she followed him, seeing with half her mind the dragon flies that swept and shimmered on its surface, and the reeds that stirred in a breath of wind. She was troubled and confused with some terrible sadness for her father, some half-understood fear that one day she too might cease to care beyond the limits of the lake, that somewhere her father had lost something precious that she still possessed. She was desperate to give it back to him.

"Father!"

She ran after him, and he turned to see her small narrow face lit up, the deep-set eyes, so like his own, blazing with a sudden excitement that was as new to him as his flood of words had been to her. She was alive after all, this daughter of his, and not as he had thought, a poor thing shrinking always from her mother's hand. Today they learned much about each other.

"Daughter?" he said, and smiled at her, surprising her into a sudden silence. The lake people did not smile.

She collected herself.

"Father, we do not have to stay at the lake, you and I."

He looked at her sharply, following her thought. "I have a tribe."

"I do not mean to leave them for always. Could we not go on a journey, you and I, and find this other world toward the sunset? Then they might come with you, if you could tell them of it. The old one knew of this far world, yet she was one of our people too. Our tribe could learn these things."

Fear snatched her breath as she spoke. What if they found the blazing light, or the gods, who must surely be of this other world, both of them? But she held her father's eye, and did not flinch from what she had said. "Can we not go?"

The father looked at her a long time, this bright-eyed girl who begged him to go searching for a world that had beckoned him when he was young, even as it beckoned her now, the world beyond the lake and the crumbling causeway, the world of the old woman. Life kindled suddenly into his eyes.

"We will go one day," he said. "One sunrise, they will find us gone. We will seek those beyond the lake who are our people too. You are right. The old one knew it."

Suddenly he laughed out loud, and tears as sudden swept to Lumna's eyes, because she had never heard him laugh before. They would laugh more on this journey to find the world.

With awkward friendliness she held him out a hand.

"Come, for now we will go to the top of the hill."

He took it almost absently.

"This world you look for," he said, "is a strange place. You could fall over it beyond the next tree."

Now it was the girl's turn to laugh, and they moved on in cheerful content, but in a few moments he turned to her again.

"I meant what I said," he said, "about the wider world being beyond the next tree. Like the old one coming to our tribe. Things are not always as far off as you think." His low forehead creased as he struggled for words that could shape thought, and not merely tell of the next piece of work. "You and I, daughter," he said slowly, "have not been far from each other all your life, yet we have not found each other until this day."

Lumna nodded, looking at him in a moment of fear and understanding, knowing that only in the light of the previous sun she herself had found the other world up here on the hill. At any moment they were going to come out of the trees onto the short turf, among the larks and the sun-warmed thyme, close to the stone that closed the cave. What if the other world was still as close at hand? She had forgotten danger in her interest and amazement in learning her father's mind. How could she tell him now that this other world might be a threat, that the choice she was making might be between his death and her own? To tell or not to tell.

"Father," she said desperately as the trees thinned, and the golden sun of the open hill struck through onto the moss and grass and small flowers in the shadows. "Father, where do the gods live?"

It stopped him. He halted and turned to her in surprise.

"The gods?" he said. "What do you know of them? Oh—the old woman. It is long, daughter, since our tribe bothered with the gods. There are none to know of them and none to tell of them. But I would think they live somewhere beyond the sun. Only the dead could tell you that."

He turned and moved into the full open sunlight, utterly unaware of her frantic fear for him; and in seconds, without sound or warning, he knew the answer to her question. There was no flashing light nor sound of terror, no hint of gods or other worlds; there was only the thin rushing whistle past her head and the spear shaft sticking from his back as he sank slowly to his knees, his last few breaths whistling like the spear itself, and the hopes of his new life fading in his eyes.

She knew who must have thrown the spear, and stood in silence above his fallen body, watching them come from the trees, Red Stripe first, his round brown face tight and his mouth compressed as one who was proved right but did not dare to say so. The men came next, drifting silently from the shadows, the boy with them shaking his head at her, and last of all the tall one, thin face severe as he gave one glance at the dead man.

"Who is it?" he asked her.

"My father," she said, and still death was not real; the suddenly small body with blood welling from its back was no concern of hers.

"You were telling him of us." The cool voice was remote and accusing. "Did I not say that you would die if you did this?"

"I was not. I was not. I could not stop him coming up the hill. He often did, to grease the stone. I told him nothing. We only came to grease the stone."

It was the little bag of grease, fallen by his hand, that brought reality, and in its limpness suddenly she knew her father's death and the final stillness of his sprawled body. Pure grief welled up in her to lose so quickly the one person she had ever thought to know. Grief over death did not trouble her tribe; a man was here or he was not, and another must be found to take his place. In

their lonely swamp they had lost touch with all the old gods to whose dwellings men went when they were dead, and whose ceremonies would have taught them how to mourn. Their dead went with small fire and sacrifice into the grave rings on the hill, with their spears and all their pots and beads, and maybe the Ancient People were there to welcome them on some far shore. But tears for death Lumna did not know. Yet suddenly they poured from her over the body of her dead father, weeping for her glimpse of a mind that saw, like her own, beyond the green lake to something more. Never again would she speak like that. Let the gods kill her now, for with her father the wider world was gone.

In a while she realized that Red Stripe and the tall one had been arguing.

"She speaks the truth," said the thin one impatiently. "When she did not tell now, she will not tell."

"Ah," said Flavius, "but what of this?" He gave a kick with his leather toe to the body of her father. "What when the tribe finds this? What then, my lord? She will tell to save her skin."

The tall young officer grimaced in distaste.

"I have no stomach, Flavius, for killing children. I am a soldier."

Flavius shrugged his massive shoulders, as though to say "What else is there to do?" There was a moment's silence. The sun flickered through the trees and splashed on bright metal, and the men's brown faces were bored and still while they leaned on their spears and waited; one death more was neither here nor there when death was your trade for pay.

Suddenly, into the sun-flecked silence, the boy spoke out.

"My lord tribune," he said clearly, so that she could understand, "I could use her."

Flavius turned to him, repressively.

"Take a slave?" he said. "Not us. The legions are rounding up the slaves to take back to Rome. Not our job."

"Not for Rome," said the boy, and she did not understand him. "For us. For my lord, I am a poor hand with the cooking pots."

For a moment the rocky face of Flavius split into a grin.

"Truth," he said, and held his stomach, and the boy turned back to Lumna.

"Has your tribe taught you other than to broil a fish?" he asked. "Can you skin an animal and use a cooking pot?"

Dumbly she nodded, the tears still wet along her cheeks, sheer bewilderment crushing grief as she struggled to know what was being said, sensing only that she was at the heart of the talk, that here for her lay life or death, tomorrow's sun or the secrets that now her father knew.

She watched Flavius lift his bushy eyebrows toward the tall thin man with the deep-colored stripes, whose long face knew only boredom and distaste for the whole business, who would be about his work, and not be bothered with children and dead savages. He nodded, however, to Flavius, who turned back to the boy.

"Take her," he said. He gave a small laugh, which rumbled through his massive body like the roaring of the ceiling in the cave. "Thus is Rome mighty, that the very slaves have slaves." The men about him laughed too and the boy grinned, and moved over toward Lumna.

"You will not die," he said to her carefully, "nor will they harm you if you do not try to run away. If you do you will die; there will be no other chance."

"Run away?" She tried to speak as carefully as he.

"Yes, now you belong to them, to me. They have given you to me to help with the cooking for the tribune. I am his slave."

Slave? Helpless, she repeated the unknown word, and he shrugged irritably, brown shoulders lifting to his fair hair.

"He took me in war. In Belga across the sea, and now I must live with him and care for him and never leave him. I do not mind. My home was burnt in the battles and I have no one else. The tribune is good to me."

Only one small word had she caught, never heard before.

"Sea?" she said.

Could anyone be so simple, the boy's face said clearly.

"What swamp do you crawl out of, girl?" he asked her in despair. "The sea. Water that ships sail on!"

She understood about water. It lay all around her home. Her face cleared a little as she grasped what after all these men might be. Gods, but perhaps from some lake such as her own in some other world. Gods, but perhaps from the far lands where the winds blew on the great plains and men knew all the secrets of the earth.

"They are gods?" she asked the boy. "Not people, these men, like you and me?"

"Of *course* they are people. They are Romans."

She shook her head. She did not believe that they were people, but she understood about the water and tried to meet him halfway.

"Lake people?" she said to him, and his deep eyes widened in horror. Lake gods was what she really meant. "Lake people! Lake people!" He looked over to where the two with stripes on their sleeves sat down together on a fallen tree, and apart to where the others were throwing themselves on the ground, easing off their metal caps and laying down their spears. "Lake people! They are *Romans*, girl! Romans of great Caesar's legions! He is come to conquer Britain, and is down there by the sea with such a gathering of ships and men as you have ever seen."

She had never seen any ships at all, nor did she understand even faintly. Were Romans people? She understood only that she must stay with them now, or she would die, be they gods or what. She gave it up, and when the boy beckoned her to follow him, she did so thankfully, with only one last backward glance toward her father. The boy, at least, was a person like herself.

Chapter Three

AT the edge of the bushes she turned once again, abruptly, and looked back at her father's body, as though to assure herself that there was no more she could do for him before she left him. He was very dead, although blood still welled from the jagged wound where the Roman had not withdrawn his spear. Lumna caught her breath again on tears she barely knew how to shed. Red Stripe sat close to her on his log, and as she turned away, she caught him looking at her with a strange expression on his face, a rough yet gentle look she did not understand, for pity was unknown among her tribe. Men lived or died and suffered with the rough care one wounded wolf might offer to another and there was no pity for the cubs. She felt confused and in some strange way safe, as if certain that this strange creature who had asked her death might also protect her. Then the boy shouted at her from the bushes ahead and she rushed to follow him.

It was evening before they stopped again, in a small clearing where the boy tumbled the contents of his leather bag out onto the grass. A piece of cheese, some bread and a couple of dead hares. He stared at them gloomily.

"Not much this evening," he said. "We have not seen a habitation all this day. There will not be much here to feed the army. The commander must look elsewhere. There has been nothing to steal."

"Army?" She echoed the easiest word he had said.

"Army," he repeated irritably. "Great Caesar goes back soon to Rome in triumph, taking hundreds of slaves from Britain, but he comes again to conquer all the land, for Rome. The tribune and his men survey the country secretly for villages and crops, and water, to know where the army can be provided for. They must eat and drink, and were they here today they would go hungry! This is no land to feed them."

Dumbly she stared at him, as he began clumsily to skin one of the hares and her mind left all the strange things he had said to watch the poor job he made of this woman's task. He looked up and found her eyes on him, and his brown face clouded with irritation.

"Sticks, girl, sticks. How can we cook without a fire?"

Lumna's spirit was creeping back out of sight of the strange creatures in leather clothes. This boy was little different from herself, for all that he shouted at her as though she were his dog, and it was on her tongue to ask him what use a fire would be to cook that animal when he had finished tearing it to strips. But fear and confusion still held her, and she turned without a word and began to gather sticks and branches around the edges of the clearing.

But when she came back with her first bundle, she looked down at him again and took her courage in her hands.

"Can you make a fire?" she asked him carefully.

He looked up, truculent, blood to his elbows from one small hare.

"Of course," he said. "Why should I not?"

"Because," she said to him simply, "you cannot skin a hare."

For a long moment he looked at her, and she looked down into the brown face a little fairer than her own, light hair tumbling to his shoulders and a longer, sharper face than any she knew in her tribe. His blue eyes were proud and angry, then suddenly they melted and he grinned.

"Can you do better?" he asked her, and she nodded, dropping the pile of brushwood and kneeling to take the knife from his hand.

On all fours he crouched a moment and watched her working with quick skill on the rest of the animal, and then he grunted.

"Woman's work," he said as though to defend himself. "I lived in a big village where there were women in plenty for this. I will do the fire."

Knife arrested in her hand, she looked at him.

"Yes," he said, stacking the brushwood with the same

44

quick skill as she showed with the hare. "Across the sea in Belga. A very big village, but the Romans overran it, and I was taken captive. They gave me to the tribune for a slave, and this is good, he treats me well." Pride was coming back after the small defeat of the hare. Pride to tell this lake savage of the world she had never heard of. "I have been with him to Rome in the last winter when he went home to see his family. There are such wonders as you never dreamed: great houses made of stone, and roads as wide as will hold ten chariots, and a huge square they call the Forum with a golden milestone in the middle that marks the center of the world. There was no need there to skin hares," he said contemptuously. "There were servants running to do all such things."

He stopped when he realized she was staring at him with her jaw dropped, dull, uncomprehending eyes peering through the fall of her tangled hair, utterly confused and understanding not one word he said; yet struggling to get some sense of his feeling for this far place. But she would not let him see her interest.

Hopelessly he shrugged.

"Savage," he said, and this she understood and anger blazed in her eyes, "but at least," he added, "you can skin a hare."

It was she who showed him again, when the fire was laid, how to notch three sticks together to make two tripods from which she hung the hares, spinning them slowly in the smoky flames, and now Cassilus looked at her in grudging admiration.

45

"No doubt," he said, "it will taste different from my cooking."

Fat dripped and sizzled in the fire and the savory smell brought Flavius and three other men in through the bushes.

"Cassilus boy," said Flavius, "you never made cooking smells like this. Are we at last to be well fed after this long time of near starvation?"

Cassilus looked offended, and the girl did not move, at ease now, crouched over a task she understood. These gods hungered like men, and with hungry men she was at home. The boy said the first thing he could think of that would take his master's admiration from this savage whose only merit was that she could cook a hare.

"Sir," he said, with contempt. "She has never heard of Rome."

The centurion raised his eyebrows, square face immobile.

"Well, Cassilus," he said mildly, "and what of that? Is that not why great Caesar has crossed this last narrow stretch from Gaul, that these barbarians may learn of Rome and come beneath her care. Why should she know of Rome? Did you, when first we overran your settlement?"

Cassilus looked put out, and Flavius grinned at him and ruffled his hair.

"Do not grudge," he said, "that she can do women's work. Is that not why we did not spit her like her father?"

Lumna did not understand, but she caught the grin

and the gesture of affection, and carefully broke off the largest joint for the man with the red stripe when she came to dividing up the hares.

Dusk was fallen by the time the meal was ready, the firelight dancing red in the middle of the small clearing, and falling on the round, brown faces of the eating men, who talked together now in the smooth-flowing speech they had used occasionally early in the day.

"These others cook for themselves," she whispered suddenly to Cassilus, looking at their separate fires.

"Soldiers," said Cassilus, and she felt more defeated than ever. The word meant nothing. "They are nothing to me," he added grandly. "I belong only to the tribune." She nodded, for what else could she do. The boy was proud of something, and after the matter of the hare it were best to let him think she was proud for him too.

After a little while she tried again, fighting against the sleep that weighed her eyelids after the long day's journey and the confusions that beset her until she did not know where to look for something that was familiar. Sleep dragged her like a refuge, but how much she wished that before she slept, there was something she could understand.

Lumna had been watching the men from where she crouched on the other side of the fire and blinked to remember that it was only with this morning's sunrise that she had left the hearth fire where she had spent so long, brooding and longing for the world outside the shredding palisades. Now in this new dusk she was far from her tribe, bewildered by things more strange than any she had ever dreamed, more beyond her understanding than any of the tales told by the old woman, frightened and strangely drawn by creatures who looked like men but were not men as she had ever known them.

Determinedly she turned to the boy.

"Are they," she asked, "from the part of the world that lies toward the sunset, where the wind blows on great plains and there are stones standing eight times higher than a man to trap the sunrise?"

He looked at her, surprised at her long speech, and then the familiar exasperation took his face as she peered at him in the dying glow of the firelight.

"They are Romans, girl. Romans, from the city of Rome, and that is toward the sunrise and not in this country. Across the sea."

She recalled desperately that the sea meant water.

"On a lake?" she asked him, and now he looked as though they had their first hope of understanding.

"On hills," he said. "You know a hill?"

She nodded, thinking of the bright, flashing lights on the far hills only in the previous daylight.

"On seven hills," the boy said then, and held up his five fingers, and then two more. "That many hills. The city stands on seven hills, and on a river, a great river called Tiber."

"Tiber," she said after him, liking the word. "Tiber."

He was pleased with her that she should try to understand, and tried to follow her in what she had said.

"I do not know," he said, "about this world toward the sunset. But when I went with the tribune to Rome, I marched with the legions down through Gaul before we took ship on the Middle Sea, and there I saw vast stones, yes, eight times higher than a man, in lines, marching over the country and the hills like great stone legions, far as the eye could see."

"We must," she thought, "be talking of the same place. We must." Her eyelids fell and she slid gently into a heap on the ground. "It is the world outside he speaks of, the world of the old woman. That is where they come from." She slept, and did not hear Cassilus get up from beside her to heap more wood onto the fire against wolves and bears through the dark hours of the night.

"Hey, Cassilus boy," said Flavius, grinning at him from across the embers. "Take care of her—you never cooked a hare like that."

"Sir," said Cassilus, firmly. "She cooks, but she is a savage." He thought of how she repeated Tiber after him. "But she will learn," he said kindly. "Already I am teaching her of Rome."

Flavius snorted, and beside him the young tribune looked up and smiled at him.

"Much good will that be to her," he said, "when we return her to her village."

"Return her?" Cassilus stood up and stared across the smoke rising from the fresh wood. "Return her?" His dismay lost him his manners to his master.

"Of course," the tribune was abrupt. "She is useful

49

while we are on this scouting party, but what then? Am I Caesar to return to Rome with a thousand captives chained at my chariot wheels to show my might against a pack of savages?"

"Sir," the centurion protested. "Go easy, Sir. Caesar is Caesar."

"And I am me," answered the tribune firmly, "and I have no use for captive children. Cassilus is well enough for me. When we go back to the ships, she will go back to her village. She will be no danger then."

Slowly Cassilus walked back into the shadows, and stood looking down at Lumna where she slept in a small brown heap, her hair fallen over her face and her body twitching a little with her dreams of marching lines of great stones eight times higher than a man and her father underneath them, nodding at her and smiling, and saying "Tiber, Tiber," as though telling her he approved of what she did.

The next day she learned a little more of what these men were doing.

In the gray morning, with mist still hanging like shrouds between the sunlit trees of yesterday, Cassilus came to her where she crouched cleaning his few simple pots, as best she could, with wet fistfuls of grass from below the trees.

She had gained courage at least with him, and she turned on him as he came up, brandishing an earthen skillet.

"You have not cleaned these," she said accusingly. "What are these Romans of yours that they eat from dirt? So great you say, but we would not eat so in our village huts, that are nothing."

He blinked and looked astonished, as though the pot itself had turned to scold him.

"Woman's work," he said then scornfully. "Now put it aside, for the tribune wants to speak with you."

Immediately she froze in fear, small face pinched like a trapped hare, her hands immobile about the pot.

"Come," said the boy impatiently, and when she did not move, he looked a moment at her face and then squatted down beside her.

"He is only a man," he said kindly. "Only a man like —like your father."

Lumna shook her head, stubbornly. He was not like her father, this thin, clean person with the long hands.

"You must come," Cassilus grew urgent. "Romans do not like to be kept waiting, even the kindest of them. He has said so."

It was not that Lumna refused to come. It was that cold, senseless fear of the unknown froze her limbs and closed her voice at the thought of coming so close to a Roman, alone, without her father. But the boy held out a hand, and something in his face told her that she must go, or she might lie herself, spitted with an impatient spear.

The tribune sat on the wet ground on his folded cloak, some sheet of pale stuff that looked like skin spread out before him in a frame, and a sharp pointed stick in his hand. One look at the child's face told him even more than it had told Cassilus.

"Come child," he said quietly and carefully, as he would gentle the colored birds in wire cages in the courtyard of his house at home. "Come here. Come close. I want to talk to you."

Near at hand, they seemed larger and stranger than ever this morning, the centurion wrapped against the chilly mist in his cloak of a red so brilliant as she had never seen before, aching with color in the gray light, making him more than ever a creature from another world.

But it was her own world they spoke about.

How long were you walking before we took you? From your village?

What does your tribe grow? Has it any animals?

And is it all forest all about your lake settlements? Any fields of grain? Any people at all?

Gradually as she understood him to be talking only of her world, her fear relaxed, and she told him as best she could the things he wanted to know. He watched her, puzzled as with everything she said, making some marks with the pointed stick on the sheet laid out before him.

In the end he stopped speaking, and stared thoughtfully at all his marks.

"We will keep to the east," he said then to his companions, in Latin. "Caesar will have to stay to the east. There would seem to be nothing here for another day's march but swamp and forest, no place to feed an army. No, it must be to the east and the higher ground."

"If the girl speaks the truth," one of the others said, hitching his brown cloak about him, and smearing the damp mist on his breastplate.

The tribune looked at her where she stood, her deep eyes flying from one to the other, fear quiet for the moment but ready to lift its shivering head. He shook his own.

"Too savage and too frightened to tell else," he said. "She does not think that we are even men. We will strike east."

They struck toward the paler sky, which told them through the forest of the strengthening sun rising to clear the mist by noon. In the days that followed, Lumna learned with slow astonishment that in truth they were like men. In spite of all their strange and complicated clothes, their brilliant colors and their handsome metals, their fine-fitting boots and close-cropped hair, she learned that they ate and slept and talked and sang and quarreled exactly as the menfolk of her tribe. But not exactly. There was a quickness and lightness in them that she had never known in the sullen silence of the lake people, an ease of speech and sudden laughter that made her in a day or two lift her own head and smile, although she did not understand the jokes that spattered out in this smooth language on the far side of the fire.

She began to know pleasure in the care of them, using all her skills in gathering herbs and roots and the woody fruits of the forest to add to what Cassilus could provide in the way of fish or game.

"They are like men," she said, watching them devour all she could find and look for more, and Cassilus looked at her as if to ask her patiently whether he had not said so.

There was a day, the third day by counting of the suns, of gray sky and rising wind, when there was much silent coming and going between the leaders and the main body of the men, much talking in quick whispers. Then suddenly she was seized and tied firmly to a tree, her wide fearful eyes fixed on Cassilus, who vanished with all the rest between the tree trunks. The man who tied her looked at her face and grinned and pointed to his stomach, but she did not understand.

There was no time to weep. The silence of their going was followed almost at once by distant shouting and the wild screaming of women and the thud and clash of weapons. Beyond the trees she saw smoke rise black and cloudy to the pale sky, and the red broken flash of flames. In a while the shouting stopped, and there was laughter in the forest and the cheerful crash of the returning men who had crept away so silently; then Cassilus, grinning broadly with two wicker baskets crammed with food: dead chickens, feathers still warm to the touch, eggs, cheese, bread, and a leather bottle filled with milk.

Cheerfully he bent down and untied her.

"Food here for a feast," he said, "and for the men, too."

Dumbly she looked at him, and thought of all she had seen.

"A village?" she asked him.

"A village," he answered cheerfully. "Well provided for. There is corn in plenty for the men to cut."

"The people?" she asked, not understanding. "What of them?"

Cassilus looked at her as if he could not believe her such a fool. Then he drew a hand hideously across his throat and stabbed another to his stomach, and Lumna understood. She looked at him, trying to grasp it.

"Killed? All of them?"

He nodded and thrust a fowl into her hands.

"Pluck it, girl."

Automatically she sent the feathers flying in a white-floating cloud, but her slow mind worked on the morning's events. In her lonely village, two generations had not seen tribal warfare, and death came only to men one at a time, by old age or accident or someone's rage. All this village was now dead, killed by these people.

Desperately she caught at the boy's arm.

"Why?" she said.

He looked at her again as though he thought her simple, which indeed she was.

"Why?" he said, "why? Great Caesar conquers Britain." Cassilus by now was more Roman than the Romans. "That is what soldiers are for! And they must eat!"

She did not understand him about great Caesar, but she looked with fresh eyes at the helmets and the metal breastplates and the leather kilts. Soldiers. The boy had used that word before. Soldiers were men who came to kill. "Soldiers are hunters," she said simply, and Cassilus looked at her now with a certain pride. She was learning. "Hunters of men," she said, and he was not sure he liked that so much.

"The Roman soldiers are the best in all the world," he said, and Lumna listened to the silence in the forest that had been a village, smoke still rising from it to the sunlit sky. From the other side came the distant noise of the men's camp where they feasted on their best meal in days, taken from the village dead.

She thought suddenly of her father saying that he and she might yet seek those beyond the lake who were also their people. Like those who had lived in this village. Prey to these mighty beings in their leather clothes. Cold anger took her with the gleam of understanding.

"Hunters," she said again, "and my people are the hunted."

Cassilus looked at her in derision.

"The legions!" he cried. "The legions, hunters! The finest soldiers in the world. They are people, the Romans —like ourselves. Does not one tribe kill another in this country? They are people!"

Sideways, Lumna looked her disbelief at him and did not speak again.

Chapter Four

THEY did not speak of it again, but Lumna was silent with the deep, heavy silence of her people, and nothing that the boy could say would break her mood. Nor would she eat the food the soldiers had so jubilantly taken from the burning village.

"Stupid," Cassilus said. "They cannot eat it now that they are dead. You might as well live on it."

"It belonged to my people," she said stubbornly, and now deeply, she knew this to be true, but could not know how to argue the rights and wrongs of war.

"And now it belongs to the Romans," the boy said irritably, and she gave him one of her direct, blue stares, thrusting back her hair.

"And you," she said, "before these—Romans—" for she could not call them people. "Before these Romans came to your land did you not live alone with your own people? Did you not get angry to see them come to kill and fire their huts and steal their food?" Some spirit was rising in her, even as the wind had risen in the last quarter of the sun until it whipped now through the thrashing trees until she had to shout to make him hear. "Did you not want to kill them?" she demanded with a ferocity that scared herself, as she looked over her shoulder at the metal armor and the long spears that would laugh at her small threat.

Cassilus looked confused. He could hardly remember a time when there had been no Romans, hardly remember the day when the marching legions had swarmed in over the flat land from the sea to absorb the big prosperous village of his tribe as though they had owned it always. Durus, the young tribune, was more real to him than the parents in his hut, whom he remembered but dimly, fair and small and faceless to him now. Rome had taken his country and was there to stay. Most of his people accepted this; he himself had forgotten there had been another life. He had seen Rome itself, and the fine home of his master, where he, a slave, lived better than the headman of his long-past village.

Confused, it all ran through his mind, but he had no words for it.

"I was small," was all he said, and turned away, making play of unrolling the bundle of his cloak, as all the soldiers had done, against the cold, rain-laden wind. "You have no cloak?" he asked her, looking at her blue bare arms. She shook her head.

"The Romans gave me this," he said, as though it proved something, but he edged up close and brought her underneath it, while they waited for the rain to cease that they might make a fire.

But all night long the rain tore through the forest, driven by wind screaming across the hilltops, filling the wild darkness with the creak and screech of breaking wood; branches wrenched from treetops, whole ancient trees heaved to the ground in a welter of smashed undergrowth and broken saplings. No one slept, nor did Flavius even give the order for the men to pitch the small tents from off their backs. All night long the soldiers huddled in their cloaks, with water streaming from the sodden leather of their helmets, until dawn came pale and colorless through the broken forest.

Lumna could hear the harsh, hectoring voice of the centurion rattling them then to their feet and compelling them to ignore discomforts, jeering at their grumbling and laughing at their hunger.

"He is cruel," she said, and the boy looked at her sharply.

He had been long now with the army.

"He asks nothing of them," he said, "that he does not do himself." He spoke as if this at least she should see. "Look, my lord is already at his work."

He pointed to where the tribune was seated on a trunk, purple cloak about him black with wet, and his thin face pale and cold after the fearful night. In the brief moment of dryness, his marked sheet was spread across his lap.

"What does he do?" she asked almost humbly, feeling suddenly and obscurely that indeed much of what he said was true, and she might be no more than a stupid savage who knew nothing.

Cassilus was glad to answer, proud of his new people.

"He makes a map," he said eagerly.

"A map?" Another new word that told her nothing.

"He marks all the places where the legions may march, and where they cannot because it is overgrown, where they may find food and water; it takes a lot of water to keep so many thousand men."

Dumbly she shook her head, and he tried again.

"All the men of the century spread through the countryside," he said, "and find these things out, and where the tribes are. Then the tribune marks them on his picture of this part of Britain, which is called a map. Then the commander can use it when he comes here in the next heat of the year. That is why we are so secret. These soldiers are not for fighting."

Hopelessly she shrugged, struggling desperately with damp wood and a wind that whipped each tiny flame away before it ever kindled.

"They are not as us," she said, and by now she was so confused that she did not know if this were good or evil. Listening to the boy, it seemed that there was no power that did not lie in the hands of these gods, and all for good. But when she thought of the burning village and her dead people, she forgot that they were gods, and powerful, and knew only thirst for the hot vengeance of the spear.

Cassilus looked baffled as he bent down to blow small helpful puffs into the bottom of the kindling to offset the gale that tore the very twigs from off the fire. How to tell her that her village in the lake, indeed his own big one on the Belgian hill, was in truth not as the great city of Rome, sprawling on her seven hills above the winding Tiber. He turned and looked at her, stubbornly staving off her hunger with a handful of hazelnuts, since she would not eat the food stolen from her people. Darkly she stared back at him, eyes brooding and distrustful under her wind-whipped hair. Suddenly he smiled and shrugged and gave it up, climbing to his feet beside her.

"No," he said amiably. "They are not as us."

There were no scouting parties sent out that day. The sodden soldiers were drying out their clothes as best they could on the trees and bushes. But she sensed a certain urgency in the centurion as the day wore on toward noon.

Flavius paced the clearing on his short, brown legs, ever and ever again glaring impatiently at the sky, as though unable to grasp why it would not obey his orders like any of his men. On the edge of the trees a thin soldier waited, watching him with an expression of tolerant patience.

"No good, centurion," he said each time he passed him. "No use. Not a flicker."

Flavius would glance once more at the racing storm clouds that were beginning to break tantalizingly here and there to gaps of pallid blue.

"Up!" he bellowed suddenly at the thin man, who looked pained and moved slowly toward a thick-

branched oak. "Up!" bellowed Flavius again, his square
face suffused with red, but the thin man grew suddenly
nimble, vanishing up into the storm-wrenched green
among the treetops. Below him Flavius watched, his
mouth compressed, his square figure rigid, and as he
stood the sun came out, flooding the sodden clearing
with pale, hesitant light. Instantly, from the high tossing
branches of the oak came the same blinding flashes that
Lumna had seen from her place beside the dwelling of

the Ancient People. Her mouth opened to a strangled scream, and she looked wildly around as though she was about to run for it. But fear of these Romans was stronger even than fear of the light. They held her with some obscure and secret terror, for fear them as ordinary people she could not; no flight could save her from them, and what would save her from the light? It was Cassilus who grabbed her, shouting at the wild blank terror of her face.

"Is it the light?" he cried, and even in the bright day, the wind tore his words so she understood only what his lips had said. Desperately she nodded.

"It is nothing," he shouted. "Nothing." He took her wrists firmly in his hands. "He has a sheet of bright metal up there and he traps the light of the sun, flashing a message to another soldier on another hill. Then he flashes to another and in no time at all the message is at the sea for the commander himself. Or he can send his orders to the tribune."

The sea, the commander, the strange senseless words that he was always using—it had no meaning for her, but at least through her wild terror she grasped that this was no more again than a thing of man. No strange possession of a group of gods. All her fear on her own hill had been caused by just such a small thin soldier up an oak tree. Trapped the sun, Cassilus had said. Her eyes were still fixed up on the top of the tree.

They watched as the small soldier shinned down again, a gray cloud sweeping up as though it knew his task was done, and they held back while he made his report to the waiting centurion, but they could read nothing on his impassive face. When he moved away toward the tribune, Cassilus beckoned to the soldier, and Lumna did not hold back when he kept her hand in his and pulled her with him.

"Come see," he said. "You will see that it is nothing." The small soldier was cheerful, brown and wrinkled as a nut, and full of good news. He chattered away to them in his own smooth tongue, and yet to Lumna's ears, which could hear a hare part grass at night a field away, it did not sound the same as when the tribune or even the centurion spoke. Perhaps, she thought, they have tribes among themselves who speak the same, but differently, as the boy and I. The Roman understood Cassilus' halting Latin, and beamed at the girl, pulling out the shining sheet from its leather pouch, and keeping a wary eye that Flavius was not watching him.

For one second, terror took the girl again as the bright metal touched her fingers. Then she grew quiet, utterly absorbed in staring into the shining surface, turning it over and back again, and raising her eyebrows and wrinkling her nose and in the end putting out her tongue, utterly unaware of the grinning boy and the man beside him.

How had they trapped in this shining sheet the image of her face that she could see in the lake water when the day was still? This held more than the sun; it held her face, as the water did, and moved when she moved. Suddenly she grew still, arrested by the blue depths of her eyes that the lake had never shown her; then in a moment she smiled a small, slow, secret smile. It was as she thought: she was not unfair to look at, fairer than her sister or the daughters of her father's brother. Abruptly she realized they watched her, both of them grinning, and she thrust it back. The Roman polished it on the end of his woolen kilt and put it away.

"Well," Cassilus said, disappointed that she had not made more of her astonishment. "You do not fear it now? It is nothing, I tell you, to many wonders of their world."

She believed him now, even if she did not understand him. How many more things of fear and terror did they know, that were too much for her simple tribe to understand? Now for the first moment, she began to understand that they might be only people. Strangers, who killed her own people easily and took what they wanted, because they knew much more. Secret things like talking from the hilltops with the flashing light. How could she get to know these things, and yet not become like a Roman as the boy had done? She saw he waited for an answer, and she glowered at him.

"I want nothing of them," she said stubbornly, her pride offended that he should have seen her delighted look at her own face. She longed to have the bright sheet again, to study her reflection for a long time, and talk to it and smile at it. To get to know Lumna herself. But she hunched a cross shoulder at the boy. "I want none of them," she said again.

They had become aware as they talked of a hum of sudden cheerfulness among the soldiers, a bustle of movement that reminded her only of the day they killed the tribe.

"What are they doing?" she demanded of the boy. "What cheers them?"

"I will find out."

He sped across the grass to where the main body of soldiers had their close-knit camp in the shelter of the trees a little off from the main clearing. They moved now in a bustle of broad grins and quick eager talk, stamping out their smoking fires and assembling in the proper order the equipment they carried rolled upon their backs. In a few moments the boy was back with Lumna, his own face as cheerful as the others.

"I'll tell you what cheers them," he cried. "The signal told them to return at once to the ships, no doubt to Rome, for they say the commander had no thought of staying longer this year. To Rome!"

She caught only the words "ships" and "sea" and always this Caesar, or commander. But she remembered something of the ships.

"They go back," she asked, "to these ships?"

"I, too," Cassilus cried. "I too. Back to Gaul, and perhaps to Rome if my lord should go too. I too."

Lumna fell silent, beating out the last glowing embers of the fire which the wind now obstinately whipped into unwanted life.

"To Gaul?" she echoed then. "To Rome?" Hopelessly she repeated the words, almost in despair. Equally despairing, Cassilus grabbed a stick and drew her over to a clean patch of earth.

"Look," he said desperately. "Look."

In the wet earth, he scratched as the tribune scratched, scoring the ground in his efforts to make her understand.

"Here," he cried, and drew a circle, "is *land*!" He looked at her. "Hills, forests, fields, people!" She nodded.

"Here," he prodded, "is sea. *Water!*" She nodded again.

"Then over here." He drew another circle. "Is more land. This is Gaul. Not your land, but across the water. So far across the water that you cannot see it. Another land."

His dark eyes begged her to understand; willed her, and at last she turned to him.

"Not my land?" He shook his head.

"Not my people?"

"No."

"What then is my land? My people?"

His face lit with excitement, and he jabbed at the first circle.

"Britain! Your people are called Britons by those who live beyond the water."

She lifted her eyes to the moving soldiers.

"And the Romans?"

"Far, far away," he told her. "Beyond Gaul and yet another sea. Toward the sunrise, on the Middle Sea."

"Water," she said.

"Yes, water."

He was impatient that the lesson went so slowly.

"Across another sea, there is a land Italia, and from there the Romans come. From Rome—"

"Tiber," she said then. "Tiber," and he smiled and let the stick drop to the ground.

"Yes," he said. "Tiber and the seven hills."

She said no more and did not look at him, shaken by the knowledge of a greater world than she had ever dreamed. Not only her own land—"Britain," she murmured thoughtfully—but other lands and other people from beyond water so wide that you could not see across it. This was too much to think and she shook her head; but clearly now was coming the understanding that these godlike creatures were no more than people from these far lands. Romans from the place called Rome. Just as she was Lumna from the lake. Not her people, nor the old one's people, but people nevertheless.

Eagerly the boy watched for her reaction, but she showed none. Slowly she turned back to her task, grinding the red embers into the soaking grass about the fire, but her slow mind, which had found little but resentment on the lonely lake, was waking to life in the quick-talking company of Cassilus, who poured into her ears these half sensed tales of a greater world. As the old one had done.

"And I?" she asked him at last, lifting her head.

Cassilus shifted uncomfortably from foot to foot, and in a moment burst out.

"Were it left to me—and I have asked my master—I

would take you. But my lord says no. He will not have a trail of children at his heels."

"Take me with you? With these Romans?"

"Take you to Gaul and then to Rome to see the wonders of their world."

Above the wet black mass that had been the fire, she stared at Cassilus with somber eyes and did not answer.

"You would not want to go?" He could not imagine such a thing.

"They killed my people." It was all she could find to say, to tell him that the new world she sought belonged in her own land with her own people and she had not found it. Only the great, incredible promises of these strangers, whom she now took surely to be men, but men that still filled her with fears for their powers and magics. That still touched her with the thoughts of gods from the other side of death. And they had killed her people; what matter what they knew, or who they were if they came only to kill all the people, so that there was no one left to know the wider world.

But all she could say again, was, "They killed my people. Am I you to run with them when they call and leave my people to die?"

Cassilus flushed a dark angry red. "I was young."

"So am I, but I will not go."

"They have many things you have never seen. Like the shining sheet in which you saw your face. To them your people are but savages."

She knew a moment of grief and longing for the

bright metal, as she lifted her hands to her face as though she would plant its shape in her memory.

"It is nothing," she said firmly. "I know from an old one of my tribe that our people knew the secrets of the sun before any Roman came into the forests with his shining sheet. Somewhere," she said obstinately, "they will know them still. I will find them."

Cassilus would have argued, his cold thin face set in obstinacy, but at that point the centurion stamped past, demanding if the whole cohort must wait upon the tribune's slave, and the boy turned away, baffled that anyone could turn so determinedly from the wonders he had seen and known. There was something about this thin girl with the long brown hair and watching eyes that made him long to take her with him, away from mud huts as he had gone himself, to a world of wide roads and houses built of stone, where even the slaves lived as she had never dreamed.

The moaning wind had whipped at the centurion's scarlet cloak, as the small fitful burst of sun that had allowed the signal faded again in the cold sky, and he stared at the small soldier reporting on his message, blank square face showing nothing of his thoughts.

"Back to the ships," he echoed, and his doubt showed in his rumbling voice.

"That's what it said," the man repeated, polishing his shining plate on the cloth he wrapped it in. "At once, at once," he added.

Flavius gave one quick glance about him through the trees to where the hill fell away to show open sky more gray and angry than Rome's deep winter ever knew. "Get back to the century," he said. "Tell them make ready to march. No delays."

The small soldier raised thick derisive eyebrows as he moved, creasing his face and dragging the warm russet of his cloak around him.

"No delays," he snorted bitterly. "Who would delay getting to the ships from this benighted place?" He drew a hand across the tip of his chilly nose. "By all the gods, I thought that Gaul was bad enough." Yet he could not resist a broad, delighted grin.

Cassilus came up to him, with Lumna by the hand to see the signal sheet, and Flavius did not even heed him, but headed smartly for his young officer who sat still before his fire, bent over his wax tablet, planning the scouting for the following day.

"Still to the north, I think, centurion," he said as Flavius came up. "To the north and east. There is a thick band of forest spreading clearly far west that would not feed a dog. Clearly to the north and east."

"No sir," Flavius said firmly, and Durus looked up, resisting the temptation to grin at the massive granite face and the terse, meager words. Whatever it was, Flavius would undoubtedly be right. The backbone of great Caesar's army, men like this Flavius, and Mars gave no man a better guide in battle. He was little higher than his width, leather creaking tight about his square, sturdy body, and had a broad face, which controlled rigidly the grin of sheer good nature that could split it with teeth white and smooth as almonds. The square, amiable face could shatter the cohort with its furious authority and the deep rumbling voice curse them within an inch of every evil fate the gods could offer, could lead them unflinchingly through fear and violence, and blood, cold, hunger, and long, fearful marches, could lead them with the same impassive grin into the very grip of death. And why not? He himself would trust his life to Flavius as he would trust it to no one else, and what matter, he thought amiably, that the good centurion believed him kindly to be a poor young fool with almost everything to learn.

Now he looked at him above his tablets, purple cloak tucked tight beneath him to stop the wind from whipping it off him like an ill-pitched tent.

"Not to the east, my Flavius?" He had to shout to make him hear, even so small a way above him. "And why?" he asked mildly.

Flavius might give his reasons, but this was his decision, and he was going to make it, even if it brought the long lower lip of his centurion thrusting out in as much disapproval as he dare show. But his face changed as Flavius answered him.

"General's orders, sir," he said. "Back to the ships, sir. At once, sir."

Durus Velanius was already rising, folding his tablets and fitting the stylus neatly into its socket, his eyes on the centurion.

"Since when?" he asked. "Bring me the messenger."

Flavius wasted no effort moving as much as a muscle until he knew what he should do. "No messenger sir. Heliograph."

"Heliograph?" The tribune looked astonished, glancing at the racing storm sky. Bent over his maps, the fleeting burst of sun had passed him by. "In this?"

"Caught a bit of sun, sir."

The wind snatched the scarlet of his cloak and whirled it around his head, but standing before his officer, he did not lift a hand to get it back. Durus looked speculatively at what he could see of his face among the blowing folds.

"Well you did," he said. "Well you did. It must be urgent. What do you make of it, centurion?"

Flavius relaxed a little, grabbing his cloak, so that he could see his officer to answer him.

"Reckon it's this storm, sir. Probably damaged the ships, sir. General has them on a shore he's never used before; can't be certain what the tides will do. Maybe a bit pressed by these savages if he's in trouble, sir. We have a whole century on this—scouting—business."

Durus looked at him gravely, but the corners of his mouth twitched, knowing the centurion was going to use a harsher word than business. He had small use for this crawling through the forest when his friends were fighting in good hot blood along the beaches.

"Very well then," he said. "Get the men moving, and we strike southeast. Get them moving at once."

Not a quiver on the tough brown face showed that the order was already given.

"And the girl, sir? Kill her?"

Good nature or not, war was war to Flavius the centurion and one enemy should be the same as any other. Secretly he thought his young officer too soft; he tried to shock him with the thought of despatching this girl. The look of distaste he expected spread over the thin face opposite him.

"What need, good Flavius? What need?"

Flavius sniffed, well aware that when Durus Velanius called him his good Flavius patience was running low.

"She'll tell, sir." He would not let him off too easily.

"And what then? We are on our way back to the ships, and will reach them before she can tell anyone."

"If there are any ships, sir. We may be held in the coast camp after this storm. The less enemy that know that the better."

Durus was as stubborn. He made an impatient gesture. "Bring her!"

When Lumna reached him, followed close by Cassilus, he had time to think about the general's order, and even his cool, chiseled face had a look of elation, dark eyes growing absent as though in his mind he had already left this bitter place for the warm, welcoming suns of Rome.

Then something about the girl alerted him, and he looked at her more closely, seeing some new thoughtfulness in the sunken blue eyes that stared at him as directly as he stared himself. Not, somehow, he thought, the blind unthinking savage that we caught. Caesar is right: we are a new world, and our very coming brings

75

civilization to this barbaric people. This one shows it in so few days.

A moment longer they stared at each other and then, "We are leaving you," he said. "If at every dawn you keep the sun on your working hand, you will then come again to your lake."

He drew himself up, and swirled his purple cloak, the might of Rome speaking to Britain in the person of this one young savage glaring at him through her brown hair with deep, unwinking eyes.

"Tell your people," he said, "that we will come again. Great Caesar is not done with Britain. Rome will straddle it as it has straddled all the world."

Her blank stare deflated him and he turned away.

"Give her two throwing spears and a bag of food," he said to Cassilus. "Turn her to the north, and she will find someone, even if she does not reach her own swamp."

Cassilus fussed unhappily as the time came to leave her. The cohort was drawn for marching, instead of their customary creeping order through the forest.

"You will get there," he assured her, assuring himself. "Keep to the north. You can use these spears."

She nodded, thinking little of him or what he said, her slow mind working on her own thoughts. Still he moved restlessly from foot to foot and looked at her and did not want to leave her, and in the end he thrust his hand down the neck of his tunic and dragged over his head a thin cord on which was threaded a small stone figure.

"Look," he said urgently. "Take this. It will protect you from harm."

Lumna looked at it lying in her palm, warm from his flesh, barely the size of her own thumb.

"Sooner I would trust my spears," she said.

"It is a god, a Roman god, who protects those who are in battle. He will care for you. Come, put it around your neck."

"Roman god," she cried. "What care I for a Roman god?" Then she stopped abruptly, staring over at where Durus spoke to his centurion before the cohort moved. The gray day blazed with the brilliant color of their cloaks; light caught in the water running down the metal of their helmets and in the flat planes of their sheathed swords. She fell silent, knowing how short a time ago she had known cold terror that these two were gods, these ordinary men who ate and slept and lost their temper and yawned and scratched like any of her tribe. No, not ordinary men, and not like any of her tribe. Romans. Not gods, but Romans, and she had begun faintly to understand what this might mean.

She took the small stone Roman god into her fingers as Cassilus dropped the cord about her head. It felt to her as if it held some of the power and strength and color of these men themselves. Romans. They would go away across this sea. But there was much she might learn first if she should follow them. Much she might learn: to tell her people.

The centurion bellowed at him, and the boy grabbed her hand in clumsy and unwilling parting. Barely she looked at him, her eyes on the soldiers melting away into the storm-whipped woods. Even when his fair, reluctant head was gone from sight, she still stood there, blinking a little, nor did she turn at once as he had told her, and keep the pinkish sky of the declining sun toward her holding hand, to guide her to her lake.

She waited until the last flicker of movement was faded from the undergrowth, and the forest left to the whining storm and the fierce determined singing of the birds who knew it must be summer, despite the winds tearing their nests apart and plastering their feathers to their cold small bodies. Then with all the skill and silence of another forest creature, a mere shadow behind the trained woodcraft of the Romans, she followed them: away from her home, the scarlet slashes of the stormy sunset away below the hillside in the direction of her working hand.

Chapter Five

ON the morning after the storm, dawn had broken on the southeast coast above the broken remnants of the Roman fleet. Coming from the tideless Middle Sea, they had no knowledge of rising tides in the cold northern oceans when the moon was full, and did not know how to clear their warships of the tidelines which smeared the rack and seaweed high along the bleak shingle shores. The wind had risen as the great October moon swung clear above the sea. It tore and shrieked as it had shrieked about the rain-soaked century in the forest, bringing with it rising, raging seas. It swept over the beached ships to rip their fittings and tear their shrouds, whipped away masts and cordage, and at last retreated slowly in the bitter dawn, like a well-contented enemy. The water-logged warships tipped and sprawled along the shore in the gray light, lying where the sea had left them, more enemy to Caesar than all the warriors of Britain, destroying transport and safety for some twelve thousand troops.

Farther out to sea, the anchored transports tore themselves loose from their moorings, and frantic soldiers lined along the shore could do no more than listen above the howling wind and seething sea to the dead destruc-

tive crunch of splintering wood, as they crashed into each other in the howling dark, or piled themselves along the shingle with the wrecked warships.

Still farther away in the pitch-dark night, the transports full of cavalry, which should have turned the expedition beyond all doubt in Caesar's favor, struggled helpless with the gale, and turned in the end to run with it back to Gaul.

With the daylight, the Commander in Chief himself came down to the shore from the camp that crowned the slight rise of land toward the inland fields. The wind still moaned from the wild gray sea, tearing the shingle backward and forward in a dull roaring, rocking the smashed hulks that still clung to the land.

Silent, Caesar marched the shore, walking with difficulty on the wet, sliding shingle, his purple cloak gathered around him, that the wind might not whip it up and take him like a sail. His small, slight figure moved determinedly from battered wreck to battered wreck, and stood a long time looking seaward at the drifting hulks of sinking ships, and toward Gaul for the sails of the cavalry that were never going to come. Finally he turned and made back toward his camp, his thin face with the calm lack of expression of a man who sets himself to quell a panic, though no panic was yet arisen in the fierce, hard discipline of Rome.

He spoke only when he was inside the Praetorium of his camp, easing the sodden leather of his helmet from his close-cropped head and letting his wet cloak slide off into the waiting hands of a slave. The tent was plain: a battered trestle table and a few leather chairs, a brazier glowing red against the mist that filled the soaking canvas, a folding bed behind a curtain. A room as simple almost as the tenting of his men.

"No one," he said then, turning sharply to his Quaestor, his Legates, Tribunes, and his Chief Centurion. "No one told us of these tides." One by one he fixed them with cold, accusing eyes.

There was nothing to be said, nor did they try to say it; they merely listened to the terse instructions from the small energetic man who walked his tent from end to end and back again, firing his orders as he walked, so that all the listening heads swung one way, then the other, on his words.

Ships there must be to get the army back to Gaul. Some ships they had, and others were in fragments. The fragments must at once be taken and used to repair all such vessels as could possibly be repaired. Any ships that were still seaworthy must be sent immediately back to Gaul for tools and materials that would be needed for this work. All troops not on guard or occupied in foraging the country for corn must be brought at once into this work. There was no question of wintering in Britain, for no corn had been provided for a longer stay.

The terse, rather harsh voice stopped. All that was necessary had been said. Caesar turned to his second in command.

"Labienus," he said, "I charge you with this small command."

He smiled suddenly, the smile of strange sweetness in

83

this small ruthless man, that made the man he ordered to his bidding feel he was doing a favor to a friend. Thus had great Caesar taken a loyal and devoted army all the way from Rome to the gale-washed shores of Kent.

"I charge you Labienus. Later I will speak to the men myself."

A few more brief and precise instructions as to the essential maintenance of the camp, and he made a gesture of dismissal.

"The century from the Seventh, that charts the land. Are they still gone?" he asked as an afterthought.

A raised eyebrow from one tribune to the other, a nod.

"Yes, sir." It was Labienus who answered.

"Call them back. I want every soldier in the camp, unless he goes for food. Signal them."

For a moment, one tribune looked again at another, but it was not for them to ask Caesar to part the storm clouds and give them sun to signal. He did not care how his orders were carried out, only that they were. Silently a tribune faded from the tent, and then all the others, leaving only Labienus and the quaestor, who must needs discuss the necessary stores.

Caesar paused in his restless walking and looked at their faces.

"Depression, gentlemen? Why so?" He shrugged, and laughed. "I promise you that it will take more than a puff of northern wind to harass Caesar. We will sail for Gaul little later than we meant."

In their expressions lay all the things they could not say to him, to the bland, self-confident eyes that watched them for the smallest show of doubt. They could not tell him that they did not share his confidence in the quick repair of the heaps of wreckage piled along the windy beach, that they looked with apprehension at the probability of a long, cold winter on these hostile shores, prey to the barbarian enemy, with little transport and less food. Caesar watched them bright-eyed, never more confident than in the cold face of disaster.

"No, gentlemen," he said again, and warm amusement lit his face as though he read their every thought. "You will winter in warm quarters in Gaul, if not in Rome itself. Now—to the ships."

The Porta Praetoria, the main gate of the camp, faced toward the green, flat spaces of the land, rising in the distance to the first ridges of the gentle hills, lost today in gray driving clouds. From it, the main road through the camp ran backward, through the tent lines of the auxiliaries and the straight rows of the legions themselves, past the canopied tent of the commander, where the eagles of the two legions held up proud Roman wings to the unfriendly British rain, past the Quaestorium, where unbelieving shipbuilders were already cramming in on to the protesting quaestor, clamoring the impossibility of what they had to do. The camp was plain and poor and small, for in his determination to make one speedy expedition to Britain before the failing of the year, Caesar had brought the legions without baggage, carrying only the fighting equipment they bore in bundles on their backs. Toward the seaward side, close against the Porta Decumana that led straight out almost to the shingle and the ships, tents had been given to the British chieftains who had come to Caesar after his first successful battle; they had come with offerings of surrender and promises to arrange for the provision of hostages as proof of their good faith throughout the winter until he should come again. They had come of their own accord, and so were given the rank of friends and were not closely guarded.

"Not that it would matter now," one sodden, blue-nosed sentry said to another as they paced the seaward earthwork, and watched the Britons gathering together in obvious excitement at the disasters that had over-taken the Roman ships. "Not that it would matter if they all bolted now. We'll have every barbarian in Britain at our throats within a day or two, as soon as word goes around we have no ships. This lot'd make small difference."

The chiefs made no immediate attempts to bolt. Through most of the day, in driving rain and fitful sun, they watched in silence the first frantic Roman efforts to reclaim their ships. They talked little among themselves, small, tawny-headed men more used to fighting each other than in banding together against the common enemy. But to all of them now, it was clear that, if this great enemy was to be driven back to Gaul from whence he had come, this was the moment that their gods of war had given them.

Through the long afternoon, while the soldiers heaved

and struggled to get all worthwhile timber above the level of the evening tide, they stood like a short, clear fringe along the earthworks, dark against the sea and sky, inimical and unspeaking, but with warm smiles and subservient nods of friendship to every purple cloak that passed.

Coming to the dusk, when the shingle was already rumbling dangerously with the rising tide, and the wind whined again more bitterly against the coming night, two tired and sweating tribunes made their way up the sliding stones toward their meal.

"Lucius." One stopped and looked, and laid his hand on his companion's arm. "We have been here all day, and so have these small fellows on the rampart. We are still here, but there are but half of them."

Lucius looked, grasping at once what the other meant. "They may be eating."

"They may not."

The fringe of small, whiskered men along the rampart was shortened now by half, nor were they in their tents, nor eating around their fires, which had been allowed to die untended.

Lucius looked back into the cold, blue evening, where the wrecked ships were piled together now, dark and desolate against the racing sky and the rising sea.

"They are gone to raise their armies!"

The cold discipline of Rome kept them walking calmly through the camp. The soldiers learned nothing from their looks other than that they had had as hard and dirty a day along the shore as the soldiers had had themselves. Fires glowed and kindled in the failing light, and smoke puffed and drifted to the rising wind, filling the evening with warm smells of woodsmoke and new-baked bread. The broad, contented chatter of the soldiers, satisfied their hard day's labor had done something toward their hope of safety, reached them as they walked.

There was no one to watch the face of Labienus when the tribunes reported to him, and it was plain with all the same anxieties that had gripped themselves when they saw the tribesmen gone.

"All of them gone?" he asked, staring at them with alarmed, assessing eyes that tried to measure the dangers of the situation. The marks of the the day were on him too: the edges of his kilt sea-soaked where he had personally supervised the struggles with the sodden timber, his lips salt-caked by the sea spray. "All of them?"

"Some half of them, sir. The rest are still along the wall."

It was the sentry on the Porta Dextra who had let them go.

"No one told me to guard them, sir," he protested, rigid to attention at being challenged by the second in command himself, chin strap framing red, embarrassed face, and brown knuckles tight and defensive around his spear. "No one told me, sir, to stop them."

Labienus sighed, tired by the sleepless, dreadful night, and the long heavy day of labor, his firm Roman face creased a little with the thought that this excuse would never do for Caesar. No smallest thing should go wrong that could not have been foreseen by someone. Should he himself, if no one less than him, have not thought that the British chiefs would immediately realize the Roman plight, and leave to raise their armies against the stranded soldiers?

He dismissed the two young tribunes, but had not even reached the Praetorium before they were back again, reporting to him that the other British chiefs had left by the Porta Sinistra. None remained now in the camp. Behind them, word had reached the legions by the strange methods with which they plucked news from out the air. No one had told them, yet word was around the fires that the hostage British chiefs were fled to raise their armies, and they, the Romans, were exposed and shipless on this open shore. Heads turned to watch Labienus, and a wordless murmur rose and blew into the dusk with the smoke above the fires, anxious faces turning back to mutter and argue in the red glow. Confidence in their commander was boundless; had he not led them all the way in victory and success from Rome itself to this almost legendary land beyond the edges of the world? Then he would get them back, in safety and success again, but by all the gods, this corner was as sticky as they had ever known. Old campaigns were raised and torn apart and fought again to measure present dangers. In food and talking they forgot reality of the bleak land that lay beyond them in the falling dark, below a sunset of torn windy scarlet, in which small men with long tangled hair were already plotting coldly their destruction.

In the Praetorian tent, all was calm and warm, braziers glowing against the salty damp, and lamps burning red along the tent poles. Caesar sat, a wine cup in his hand, bathed and fresh after the anxious day whose labors would continue all the night, by the light of torches flaring in the wind, amid great piles of blue-flamed drift and broken timbers. He lounged against the colored cushions of his couch, as though his campaign were safely over and all its battles won.

"Well, Labienus friend," he cried. "Take wine with me. How went the day for you? Well, I think for all of us. They performed prodigies of labor, my good men, and as soon as possible, we will get all we need from Gaul and put the sound ships to sea again. No time at all."

It was this boundless confidence that had conquered half the world, and was ready to move on and conquer all the rest. In its aura, Labienus relaxed a little, losing the memory of the wave of anxiety that had followed him through the legion's tents as clear as the rain that drove across the fields.

"Take wine with me," said Caesar, "and tell me all your news."

Labienus took the silver cup from the slave standing by the wall, framing its cool carving with his hands, and framing the words he would use to break his news to his commander.

"The day went well, sir. As you say, they performed miracles down on the shore." He did not add that well they might, as the army knew it was their lives and safety that they worked for. "But the evening not so well."

Bright eyes sharpened over Caesar's wine cup, but he did not move, waiting for the other man to finish. He was not one to waste his words in idle comment over facts not given.

Labienus could not find way around it.

"The British chiefs are fled, sir," he said bluntly, and waited for the storm.

"Well?"

Could the commander possibly be so foolish as not to understand what this would mean? Labienus' hard brown face creased with disbelief.

"Well, sir," he said carefully, lest he be telling Caesar something he already knew, as was all too possible, "they will have gone to raise their armies against our position here, while we are defenseless."

"Of course. What else would they do, unless they were fools?"

"You let them go?"

"I let them go. What avail to keep them? They were only extra mouths to feed when food is short. I made no attempt to hold them. If they had not gone, word would soon have reached the tribes in any case, and their armies would have come without them. No, let them go." He laid down his wine cup on the table, and the colored cushions went flying with the energy of his rising to walk the room, as he always walked when he was thinking.

"No, Labienus, I foresaw that this was about to occur as soon as our fleet was damaged. This is what any commander in their place would do. We will make no more sorties from the camp, but keep all our men here for the labor on the ships for every moment they can be spared. If the Britons come, then we will defend the camp, and be well placed to do so, with all our strength inside it. But corn we must get every day." He paused before a chart hung on the tent wall. "Corn we must have, and close by in this district; stocks are running low."

He turned sharply to Labienus.

"The century we sent prospecting is not yet back?"

"No, sir. In the late day of tomorrow I would think."

Caesar grunted, still looking at his chart. "Let us hope they have something to tell me that I do not know."

Labienus doubted it, but at that moment Caesar turned, with a friendly smile and talk of Rome, and the military matters were at an end.

The day that followed was of a wind-washed brightness, as though the storm had burnished the very world —clear blues and greens and purples striping the restless sea, and small tattered clouds whipping across skies as blue as those above the hills of Rome. The beaches and the flat fields about the camp echoed to the crack and thud of hammers as the legionaires strove to spring the trap the storm had made for them. Out to sea stood clear the brown sails of ships fit to sail to Gaul for more supplies.

Special observers had been sent on horseback out through the country inland from the camp, where in the quiet days since the successful battle the tribesmen had come back to their work in the fields about the villages. By the end of the bright day, when they cantered back into the camp, they told Caesar again what he already knew. The tribes were gone once more from the fields, sloping empty and untended up the gentle hills, and again around the evening fires the soldiers looked at each other, and laid bets for themselves as to the race between the mending of the ships and the gathering of the small tawny men in their secret places in the far forests.

It was clear, shining dusk, with the sunset yellow over the darkening land and all the light of evening still lying in the sea, when the century in charge of Durus Velanius came in the last straight stretch across the fields to the Porta Praetoria, marching at the steady legions' tramp that had brought them all from Rome and would bring them there again, Cassilus thumping valiantly behind their heels. They had avoided villages, and taken the deserted tracks found on their way out, and had seen no signs of gathering tribes, nor any preparation to attack the camp.

"No, sir. Nothing." Durus stood tall and calm in front of Labienus, to whom he must report, his helmet under his left arm, his mind whirling bewildered under his calm face, at the destruction he had found on his return to camp.

"Corn, sir. Yes, sir." By Jupiter, he thought, they'll have need of corn to feed them while they put this lot right. A pace behind him, the granite face of Flavius showed a certain disgust at a pack of soldiers who could not be left to look after a few ships without letting them get smashed up.

"There is one large area of still-standing corn, sir. To the northwest, some two hours march. Perhaps a little more, for the tracks are not good." The legions' time was measured on their own metaled roads, where the steady thump of feet could cover twenty miles a day. "This is the only standing corn that is left in all this area, sir."

"Enough, you think, to feed the two legions until the ships are ready?"

Labienus could not help thrusting a little of his anxieties on the younger man, and Durus shrugged faintly, as though to say, I am not the quaestor.

"It is all you will get sir. There is nowhere else."

Labienus nodded and dismissed him. Gathering up the plans the young tribune had brought him back, he went to the Praetorium to Caesar.

Caesar pulled his lower lip, and stared at the plans spread out on the carved top of his record chest. Lamplight was warm and yellow on his face, and light splintered from the shining gold of his embossed breastplate, hanging beside him on its stand. In the tent there was small air of the danger of destruction and starvation that threatened the men about the fires outside. Nor was there any of it on the commander's face when he laid the parchment down.

"Enough," he said firmly. "Enough. It will suffice for as long as we will take to repair the fleet. So long, no longer, but we must have it all. Labienus."

"Sir."

"We must spare some of the men from the ships, to go for this corn. A good number so that all of it may be gathered at once. Enough to look after themselves also, since it is some distance from the camp."

"Two cohorts, sir?"

"Three."

He turned to the chart showing the disposition of cohorts of the two legions. In the silence, from the windy dark outside, the trumpets split the night calling for Last Rounds, and at the Porta Praetoria the torches of the centurions flared and sputtered as they waited for the Tribune of the Watch.

"The Seventh," Caesar said, stabbing a short, fine cut finger at the plan. "Three cohorts of the Seventh Legion. Detach them at dawn for gathering in this corn."

In his own quarters, with the other slaves and camp followers, Cassilus stretched his weary muscles, and rubbed his feet, for the legions took no heed of shorter legs than theirs. He was almost too tired to understand the damage of the storm and the danger to the troops, but left it all to his unfailing confidence in his Roman masters. As he eased his feet back into his sandals, his eyes were absent on the blue-flamed fire, and his mind on the picture of a small slight girl, staring after him through tousled hair, her hand still up to hold his small stone god. He had an uneasy, formless feeling that she had never turned for her lake home, that she would not easily do as she was bid. There will be fighting now, he thought anxiously, now that the legions cannot get away. Of course there will be fighting. Were she better to have stayed with us, or at home? Where were she better to have stayed?

His tired mind could worry no further, sleep sliding over him as the rising tide slid up the cold, moonlit beach below. Despite the flaring trumpets and the noise, he was still asleep when the three cohorts of the Seventh Legion marched out into the shadowed fields with dawn flaring red behind them over a purple sea.

Chapter Six

LONG before dusk, Lumna knew that she had lost the Romans, her skilled movement through the forest being no match for long, hard-trained legs that were concerned now only to reach the coast as fast as the ground would let them march.

By the next day, after another cold, unhappy night, perched in a great oak, she knew that she had lost herself. Keep the sun, they had said, to your holding hand, and that will face you home. But although the wind had died, she was still in the forest when the gray dawn barely changed the color of the night, the clouds hanging so low and still above the trees that it was impossible to know where the gray spreading lightness had begun. Even when she found herself clear of trees, walking the ridge of low, bare hills, it was too late to find the sun. Chilly, even light filled all the sky, no more in one part than the other, and she wandered aimlessly, a small brown figure in an empty world, toiling along the long, green shoulder of a hill, whose final crest was dark and crowded with a grove of oaks. There was no sound about her but the soft keening of wheeling lapwings, and the shrilling of one solitary lark that like herself was struggling toward the sun.

She was tired and full of fear, alone in the desolate misty world to try and sort for herself all its mysteries and strangeness—all the new knowledge that had been thrust at her in these last days. She had not even the security of the lake, nor the comfort of being close to her own Romans, as she now thought of them. How much gods and how much men? How much fearful magic, and how much, like the flashing light, of things quite simple that her own people were too savage to know?

When the first acorn struck her, she did not know what it was, brushing at her forehead as though a fly had touched her. But another hit her hand and then her leg, and then another full between the eyes, which angered her, and woke her from her dreaming. She looked at them falling around her on the ground. No magic this, but acorns, still a little green, being pelted at her from the grove of oaks, a short way above her on the steepening slope. Angrily she rubbed her stinging nose, and took a spear into her throwing hand, pausing a moment to feel its weight, and something unaccustomed in its balance. A Roman spear. She had not thought of this, and almost dropped it, to look in curiosity at the smooth-honed shaft and rounded head. Then another acorn hit her and with it came a burst of

98

laughter from the trees, girls' laughter, young like her own, though laughter had not been heard much on the lake.

"Drop the spear," a voice said then. "We do not harm you." Again, the words were not as her own tribes spoke, nor yet as Cassilus, but she understood, and then she saw them, five girls sitting and lying around the bottom of an oak some small way inside the shadows of the wood. Five girls, some older, some younger, not Roman, all fair or tawny like herself. They were not Romans, so surely they must be her own people: that she and her father would have sought. What harm could come to her? Carefully she dropped the spear, and made her slow way toward them, blue eyes cautious, for she was not yet sure. But the girls only pealed with laughter once again.

"Come, sister. What is there about us so fearful? Who are you? And why are you wandering here alone?" This the eldest, in a tunic of the color of the trees, fair hair tangling over it almost to her waist. Still Lumna did not speak, standing looking down at them as though they were as strange to her as the Romans in the secret place.

"There is nothing to fear," cried another, and the small ones laughed at nothing and tumbled on the tree roots like a pair of puppies. "We are only here to mind the pigs. We have no weapons like you. We are not Romans!"

They thought this the greatest jest of all, and shouted their amusement that they, the pig girls, might bring someone to the same fear as the terrifying tales of this armored enemy that had arrived along the sea coasts. "We are not Romans," they cried again, and now Lumna spoke.

"Romans?" she demanded. "What do you know of them?" And now they all stopped laughing, even the small ones staring at her in alarm with big eyes still damp with mirth, for there was some strange ferocity in her voice, some fierce determination in the eyes she fixed on them. And she did not speak as they did. This halted them.

Slowly the eldest scrambled to her feet, brushing the mold and dead leaves from her tunic, and pushing back her hair.

"Who are you," she demanded then, "that you come alone to our village bearing spears? And you do not speak our tongue."

"No matter who I am," Lumna retorted, and moved a spear back into her throwing hand, her eyes never leaving the big blue ones of the fair-haired girl. "Tell me of the Romans." What others could they be than the ones she was following? If she could get words out of this foolish creature she might yet catch them up. For a moment, the woodland and the girl were blotted out by a sudden picture of the high-cheeked knobby face of Cassilus, and Lumna felt alone and tired. Hot, un-accustomed tears pricked at her eyes, and drove her to anger because she did not understand them, but the girl had understood the gesture with the spear, and so had her sister behind her.

"Tell her, tell her," the younger one cried, "or she will kill us all. What matter what you tell her of the Romans?"

The taller girl stared at Lumna, unable to understand her anger, or the sudden tears that had filled her dark blue eyes, but like her sister, she was not going to chance being spitted to a tree for something she cared nothing for.

"Hold your spear, girl. Why should I not tell you of the Romans? Does not everybody know that they have come from Gaul to conquer Britain, and are down there on the sea shore with ships and men in such numbers as no one has ever seen. Dressed in metal, they say, and carrying their gods before them as they march, on high poles so that all can see them. Tall men, as high as twice my father and very fierce, and full of arms, and they are set to kill us all. Now do you know about the Romans? I did not think there was anyone did not."

Puzzled, she watched Lumna's spear hand dropping, and weariness fill her disappointed face.

"Is that not what you wanted to know?"

Lumna blinked at them. For days she had thought of nothing but the Romans, wrapped in her confusion as to whether they were gods or men, while this crowd of laughing girls took them for granted, just as an ordinary enemy, but used all the same words that Cassilus had: ships, and sea and men such as she had never seen.

"Are you not afraid of them?" she asked.

"Oh yes," they chorused. "Oh yes," and the small ones stared from one to the other with great frightened eyes. "If they come they will kill us all except the strongest, and they will take them back to the fearful land they come from to work forever, and they will never see their homes again. And they will take our land as they have taken all of Gaul for their own."

Watching their changed faces, and the hands that strayed to grip each other as they talked, Lumna could see they were indeed afraid, but not as she had been. They feared an ordinary mortal enemy such as the old woman had described sweeping down on her homestead in the far plains, whipping away the women and children in a welter of blood and burning thatch. These were not the things she had feared, perhaps because she had never seen a real, ordinary enemy, but the old one had filled her head full of ghosts and gods.

She creased her forehead, trying to sort it all.

"Rome," she said then absently, answering one part of what the taller girl had said, and saw them staring at her.

"Rome," she said again. "The land they come from. And it is not fearful. The people live as we have never dreamed, in great stone houses." Her face grew gentle and her eyes distant, as she repeated the words of Cassilus over the evening fire, words she had pretended that she didn't listen to, asking him why she should wish to know of Rome. Now she realized they were looking at her with nearly the same haunted superstitious fear as she had offered the Romans.

"How do you know?" the eldest asked, almost in a whisper.

"How do I know?"

She looked at their frightened faces, and could not resist to boast a little.

"I have been with them," she said, aloofly. "For several days."

Clearly they did not believe her, staring. Then the faces of the older ones changed to the expression she knew so well in her own village. Contempt for Lumna, with her head full of foolishness. The oldest began to laugh.

"Oh," she said derisively. "You were with the Romans and you are here to tell us of it! This I do not believe. They took you captive?"

Already all the events of the last days were becoming like a dream, difficult to remember and to sort out into words. There had been no captivity as these girls might know it, no ropes and bonds, only the fearful promise of death, in which she had believed.

"I went with them," she said lamely, and the girl laughed again. This time the small ones joining with their treble hoots, taking courage that the Romans did not after all seem to be so close.

Lumna grew angry. Her lips tightened and she thrust her spearhead close against a grinning face.

"Look close at that," she said, as the affronted girl drew back. "Look close at that and tell me if you have seen such a one before?"

Down her nose, leaning hard against the tree at her back, the girl looked closely at the spear, and now the others did not laugh.

"You were truly with the Romans?" she said then, and suspiciously, "why?"

Lumna shrugged. "They said they would kill me if I ran away, and they meant it." She saw clearly the square granite face of Flavius, who would have spitted her without a thought.

The fair girl thrust the spear aside, her eyes on Lumna with some new respect.

"Come to my father," she said, and when Lumna drew back, she took her arm and shook her.

"There is something with these Romans," she said urgently. "They are in some trouble with their ships. Our warriors are sharpening their spears, to catch the enemy the moment he is helpless, and they will kill them all."

Now Lumna laughed, remembering the close-fitting armor and the metal helms, the tight, ordered discipline, and the firm resolute faces. She fingered her Roman spear and thought of the village in the forest, and what had happened when the soldiers needed food. These people, who must be like her own family down on the lake, to kill all the Romans?

"You have not seen them," she said, and shook her head.

The girl urged her on. "No matter. You will tell my father all you know."

Lumna shrugged again, and went with her quietly, the little ones hopping and dancing around the edges of the group, the pigs forgotten in among the oaks, in some sudden urgency that gripped the oldest girl.

Lumna looked at her calmly and without hope. What help would it be for her to tell anything? And what matter what she told? It would make no difference. Her words to Cassilus came back into her mind.

"Soldiers are hunters, and our people are the hunted." Her Romans could kill all these simple people as they had killed the people in the forest. This was what she would tell them: her people.

Long before she reached the girl's father, she had begun to wonder in deep bewilderment if she were wrong. It was to no lake village, crouched in loneliness and silence that she was led. Beyond the thicket of oaks, the land rose sharply to the narrow crest of a hill ringed with wooden palisades, three rings, from the first slope above the forest to the top, where thatched roofs showed above the walls. When they climbed to the first fence, Lumna gazed in silence at the deep ditch dug inside it, the earth piled to make an added barrier below the wall. There was no way through, and the girl signed to her to follow around the wall to the other side of the hill.

Here the land fell away more gently and the green hill widened out. Lumna lifted her astonished eyes up the slopes, past ring on ring of stout defenses, to the roofs of the big village that covered the high crest and flooded down the slopes between the palisades—thatch in all the colors of its age, from honey gold to rotting black. Not all the dwellings were small, and her mind tried to grasp the size of some of the buildings that must spread beneath such rooftrees.

The girl pulled her on, indifferent to her amazement, never thinking that one who had been dwelling with the Romans would be tipped beyond the balance of her understanding by a hill-fort of her own people.

But Lumna was speechless in bewilderment, groping dimly back to all the feelings that had driven her angry from her home. This must be her wider world. No need to go to Rome for it. Here was the world the old one had spoken of. Astonishment filled her, and sudden

delight, untouched by the superstitious fear that had gripped her with the Romans. Her world, and her people. In her heart she had known that they were not all like the dull and sullen people of the lake. The old one and her father had been right.

She knew chariots when she saw them, wheeling and turning on a flat stretch of field inside the second wall. The old one had told her clearly of these, of the bright colors and the wheeling snorting horses and the shouting men, whips cracking in the bright air. On all sides men were gathered in great numbers, more flooding through the gates in groups and ones and twos, all carrying their spears and clubs and wicker shields, many of them mounted on sturdy horses which they rode lightly and thoughtlessly, as if they were part of the animal themselves.

The girl turned to Lumna and caught her open mouth and her astonished face, and she stopped, looking at her curiously.

"You have known the Romans," she said, perceptively, "yet you look amazed at your own people. What is it?"

Hastily Lumna closed her mouth and masked her whirling mind with a look of boredom.

"Nothing. I only look at their arms, and think how they will meet the Romans."

Not to tell this superior girl that she was as helpless with confusion as if Cassilus had taken her and put her down in this Rome itself that he clearly thought so much of.

"And will they?" the girl said sharply.

Lumna shook her head, though already uncertain of what she said, but at least she had begun to understand that her Romans were only a small number out of many, that somewhere, beyond wide water, there were Romans in numbers more vast than she could dream. No small, sturdy, hill men with their spears and even with their chariots could match so many Romans. They would be killed even as the others. This was what the Romans came for.

She could not help stopping to stare again as they reached the last high circle of the palisaded hill, a wide open space ringed with thatched huts and ancient trees, in its center a huge circular building with wooden pillars holding up the roof. A palisade of its own fenced in a space around it, with some shapeless standing stones and great black yew trees, solid against the high sky.

Pride struggled with curiosity, and she could not keep from asking, "What is that?" This time the girl did not sneer at her, coming close to speak softly.

"The temple," she said, and looked at her sharply. The old woman's words again. Before the girl could go on, she spoke herself, gazing at the wooden building with a sudden knowledge as though she had known it all her life.

"The gods live there," she said, dredging her mind for all she had been told.

The girl nodded, fair face quiet and a little fearful.

"They will sacrifice tonight to Nodens, and to Canopus who is the god of youth, for it is the young who die in battles—and the old must go to the gods and speak for them."

She had an air of saying something that had been already said to her, and Lumna looked at her, waiting for more, but the girl snatched her hand and rushed her on across the open space between the milling men, to the largest of the huts on the hilltop.

Men were crowded about the dark entry, moving and talking and regrouping to talk again, their thin faces alight with the excitement that Lumna had sensed the moment they had entered the bottom gate. Spears lay in stacks against the wattle wall and crossed spears barred the girls from going beyond the door. A young man with thick brown hair and short legs detached himself from a shouting group and came toward them angrily.

"What are you doing here?" he demanded. "Have you lost your sense? This is a council of war, and not a woman's feast! Get gone, I say. Get gone at once."

He did not even look at Lumna nor question that she was a stranger. One girl more or less in the teeming fort was nothing. The fair one grasped a fistful of his bearskin tunic, holding him lest they should lose him.

"Oh, brother, not so speedy! This is why I am here, that it is a council of war." She looked all around her at the falling silence, and the faces that had begun to turn and watch this strange scene of two women at the chieftain's door, with the sharpened spears against the wall and the enemy waiting down below on the open shore. The wind sang in Lumna's ears and whipped at her hair, nor did she know where to face to move away from all these watching eyes. Frantically she plucked at the green tunic of the other girl.

"Let us go," she whispered urgently.

The girl took no heed, but grabbed her brother closer by his long fur and hissed fiercely into his ear, both their eyes now on Lumna, the young man's in derision first and then open laughter.

The girl stamped.

"It is true," she said. "True. And you waste time not to tell my father." She had forgotten to whisper, and now the curious men were crowding closer. "She was with the Romans. See her spear."

The young man seized a spear, cast her one fierce questioning glance above it, and turned the iron head within his fingers.

"It is not ours," he said, and the fierce, brown eyes came around again to Lumna.

"What do you know of them?"

"Much, much," she cried. "You cannot defend yourselves against them!"

How could she let these her own people be slaughtered as the tribe was slaughtered in the forest? But even as she spoke a silence fell around her, and broad smiles creased the weatherbeaten faces, and men began to turn away. More women's rubbish. All the fort was packed as it was this evening because of the messages from the fleeing chiefs that great Caesar lay at Britain's mercy, helpless and defenseless on an open shore. Victory was theirs now, and they would hear of nothing else.

But the young man seized Lumna by the hand.

"You will tell my father all you know," he said, pulling her toward the crossed spears, which he struck down with one sharp gesture. They closed again across the furious face of the other girl, and Lumna found herself in a vast crowded hut, larger than she had ever seen. Smoke poured to the blackened rafters from a huge fire in the middle of the floor, and men crowded every space with packed, sweat-shining bodies, so that it was all the youth could do to drag Lumna through them to where an old man sat on a bench, piled high with skins, his gray hair falling on a tunic of the same aching color as the young Roman's in the forest.

Excitement took her in the noise and turmoil, caught from the smoke-filled air so full of urgent talk, so that she faced the old man with bright, blazing eyes, as ready for battle as the warriors, who worked on the edges of their spears.

"Yes, I have seen them," she cried, when the youth had managed to silence those about his father, and take his whole attention. "I have been days with them and seen their ways, and know them."

Fear left her, even as a listening silence filled the hut, rustling with murmurs of respect and curiosity. Messages only had come from the chiefs who fled the camp. Scouts had watched the Romans from a distance, but no one in the fort had ever seen them close at hand, and men four times her age crowded to Lumna, seeking her young words. Her high cheekbones flushed and the blue eyes blazed at them.

"I tell you," she cried, "that you cannot fight them!"
A deep murmur rose from the men, like the growling
of the kenneled wolfhounds in the night.

"And why not so?"

The old chief was the calmest of them all, not yet
worked up into the passion of battle, which kindled
all his tribe. Lumna stumbled over her words to answer
him, her mind full of the massacred village in the forest.

"They have—they have," she paused and looked at
her spear, unable suddenly to tell him what it was the
Romans had that had made her think of them as gods,
that filled her with the certainty that these shouting
warriors on the hill outside were just as children,
sharpening their wooden spears beside her lake home.
These things she hardly thought, nor had she words
for them. "They have better spears," she said lamely,
unable to find the words for discipline and order and
precision, and all the fierce training of the legions.

The old man brushed it aside.

"Tell me," he said, "what they were doing in the
forest."

Now she rushed into words. These things she could
tell them of, and it might stop them charging from their
fort to hurl themselves upon the Roman spears. She told
them of the signal lights that passed the messages of the
legions all across the land, told them of the making of
the map, and the searching out of corn.

"Corn," said several voices all together, and she saw
them look at each other in sudden wild excitement.
"Corn?"

"Yes. It was the tribune's duty." Self-important, she brought out the words she hoped they would not know.

"Tell us of the corn," they demanded, and now the faces around her were intent and fierce. "Tell us of the corn."

She told them, of the planning of all the cornfields that the legions might be fed, and now she spoke of the legions as if she had known them all her days. "They live on corn," she said, explaining it carefully, unaware of the glances that passed above her head from man to man. "They must have corn to feed the soldiers."

"Take her away," the old man said suddenly, and now his calm was gone, and excitement broke his voice. "Take her away." His eyes blazed at those about him, as though no words need be said and they would know his thoughts.

"Corn," he said. "Corn."

As Lumna was dragged out through the men who crowded around him, their voices were rising in a roar of triumph, beating each other about the shoulders and taking each other's arms. Confused and troubled, she looked back at the mass of cheerful faces until she was clear of the hut. She did not understand their mood. She thought she had told them enough to terrorize them, to keep them safe inside their strong fort until the Romans went away, for who were they that they could fight them, any more than the poor people in the smoking ruin in the forest?

Outside, the chief's daughter waited for her, but Lumna looked at her from her deep blue eyes, confused, and unable to answer when the girl asked what her father had thought of all she said.

The last boisterous remnants of the storm were dying out, and the great trees along the hilltop had grown still, clear sky paling toward a perfect evening, the quiet air heavy with the wheeling thunder of the chariots and the sonorous murmur and movement of a thousand men.

Chapter Seven

Darkness crept up on the teeming fort. The last light faded from the far western sky and the great gibbous moon swung up above the hill, bleaching the high slopes and paling the flaring scarlet of kindling torches.

On the lower slopes, the horses had been unharnessed and the fierce, painted chariots stood in rows, knives gleaming vicious at their wheel hubs. The sharpened spears were stacked in piles and skin shields laid down beside them, men coming one by one to leave their arms. Moonlight and fire mixed on their faces, all held in a strange falling silence that yet kept their eyes from one another in a tension and excitement rising like incense to the hilltop, where the first red flames licked about a great fire piled in the courtyard of the temple.

Lumna, in the women's hut, heard the falling silence, and saw the women look at each other in the smoky darkness, their expressions strange as the growing quiet beyond the wattle walls.

"What is it?" she asked the chief's daughter; there was something in the women's eyes that made her whisper. Excitement and with it fear, and the same awe that had touched the girl's face when she and Lumna had passed the temple.

The girl looked at her, and only then did Lumna think that she had never asked her name. The fair girl. The oldest one.

"What is it?" she said again, and now the silence was as palpable as the mist that crept about her lake. "What happens on the hill?"

The fair girl shook her head, as though she denied that she must even speak of it.

"It is not for us. No woman must leave the huts tonight," she whispered, and in the dead quiet and the awestruck faces, and the knowledge of the men crowding for some secret purpose on the hill, Lumna heard again the voice of the old woman in her home, whispering in secret of things she swore she should never know. This then was her world. No vast distance to the sunset, but a few days march and a hill or two from the forgotten lake.

"But what?" she whispered to the girl, teased since childhood by these half-whispered secrets. "But what?"

The girl looked at her again and glanced at the older women around the fire.

"My brother told me," she whispered. "At dawn they will attack the Romans. Tonight," she added in a voice that told she would say no more, "is for the men and the gods."

The men and the gods. Lumna peered around at all the faces ringed about the fires, intent upon the evening food and yet alive with sideway glances and listening looks, and a strange furtive triumph and excitement. Suddenly, in this hut that was much larger, but as smoky, dark, and evil-smelling as her home, in the hum of whispers and the clatter of pots, cold creeping fear pricked along her skin and ran like fire over her scalp.

Desperately she locked her hands together and tried to know for whom she was afraid, bewildered that the only pictures in her mind were the bony cheekbones and the awkward kindness of Cassilus, the great white grin of the centurion, and, foolishly, the long, clean, brown fingers of the young tribune, delicately marking the smooth wax of his map.

"No!" she cried out before she could stop. "No," and the girls about her looked at her curiously.

"Nothing," she mumbled. "It is nothing." And indeed it was nothing, as she thought about it, the clammy sweat drying on her hands and her face relaxing. There were Romans in vast numbers, half gods still to her. These savages could not defeat them. Astonished, she found herself using the word that the centurion had used of herself, which had driven her to anger. Guiltily she looked around as though they might have heard her thoughts. Savages. Even Cassilus had said this. These were her own people. This was the wider world she had dreamed of, in her own land, the world she had longed to go and find—her father's world. Yet she wanted to see them as she had seen the other tribe, slaughtered by the flat Roman swords. Or did she?

She felt as vague and formless as the smoke drifting to the roof hole, spreading and lying among the rafters in the still night.

"Lumna," she said, as if to tell herself whom she was, and where she came from. "Lumna." Desperately she looked around the great hut grown suddenly intolerably hot, and leaped to her feet, full of the urgent need to leave these people before she was one of them. Out alone on the hills, she would be only Lumna; she would belong to no one, have no sides to take in this battle, feel no frightened grief for slaughtered Romans nor guilt that she did not belong with these, her people. Gods, savages, people, who or what they all were she felt beyond her knowing. Nor should she be asked to choose, she did not understand. She must go, to be alone and be only herself with no care for any of them.

They jumped with her as she leaped to her feet and in a wild stampede made suddenly toward the door. Hands grabbed her tunic and dragged her back, shocked faces under their long tangled hair, with wide angry eyes, crowding at her on all sides like a terror of her sleep. Firelight shone on them and lamplight from the walls, and the smoky shadows fell on them, and their opening and closing furious mouths that she could not understand, and suddenly they were more terrifying than any cool strange threat from the Roman soldiers.

"I must go," she shouted. "I must go!"

They were rough with her, incredulous that she should behave so, pushing her back to the fire and thrusting her down on her heap of skins, the fair girl looking at her as if she had taken leave of her senses.

"They would kill you," she said, staring at Lumna, amazed that she could not understand this. "They would kill you." The other women had drawn back, still staring and muttering and the girl held Lumna's hands and looked into her wild eyes. "Have you never known such a night?" She would not say more, and Lumna could only shake her head, tears of confusion and distress and pain from her pulled hair hot and sharp against her eyes. "Such a death," the girl went on, her eyes turning toward the walls. "Listen."

There was no longer silence out beyond the walls. Instead there was a sound like the honey bees that her tribe had kept in the sheltered meadow at the lake edge, swelling as they listened to it to a great rumbling roar. Silence now lay only in the hut, and above the formless thunder of men's voices they could hear the crackle of the huge temple fire on the other side of the hilltop, drowned out in the end by a roaring and shouting that seemed to press against the vast hut as though it were as fragile as the lake reeds, ready to crumble under the rising fearful torrent of sound.

Lumna could see nothing; no woman dare as much as part the curtains of the door, and she could only stare wide-eyed at the walls that held out the fire and the darkness and the noise of a thousand feet stamping and circling on the hilltop. She saw no fires, nor the dread bull-headed masking of the priests, nor the broad flashing knives of sacrifice red with firelight and with blood. Only she heard the endless shouting and the strange unearthly chants, the reedy fluting piercing the noise like pain, and then thin terrible screaming that she did not understand, making the women look at each other underneath their hair, unwilling to be weak.

In the last hours of the long night, when the cracks of the curtained door showed the blackest hours before the first gray light, and the noise was at its wildest, she heard the thunder of chariot wheels on the hill below. The thumping of bare feet outside took pattern, moving down the slope, and the clash of spears drowned out the thin wailing of the music.

In a while the noise was gone from about the temple, loud and urgent now, but with a different note, farther down the hill, and in the new silence one of the women crept to pull aside the curtains of the door. The first thin light of day was threading the dark, and Lumna, peering over her shoulder and longing to escape, saw the fire before the temple burned low to glowing ashes and the dark doors closed on silence.

The woman turned, and her tense face broke into a sudden laugh, strong white teeth gleaming in the firelight. As though at a signal, tension and silence among the women broke, and all but the oldest began to laugh and chatter, pushing and thrusting for the door and the first chill daylight.

"What now?" she cried bewildered, thrust back toward the fire in the urgent rush.

Beside her the fair girl reached over for a spear, her blue eyes wide with excitement she seemed to have been saving all the night. She stood over Lumna with the firelight in her long hair and stared at her with the same expression as Cassilus had done, as if to ask could anyone be such a fool.

"What now?" she cried. "Now the battle!"

Lumna still stared, and by now they were alone in the huge hut, save for a few toothless old ones mumbling by the fire.

The girl shook her spear.

"Your spear! We go to the battle!"

"Women! I thought battle was for warriors?"

The girl laughed, and ran her red tongue around her lips, seeming to have taken on a sudden wildness.

"First we watch," she cried. "Then when they need us, we fight. They say it will terrify these Romans, whose women do not go to war!" She laughed again, and then looked impatiently beyond the door at the growing light, and listened to the thunder down the hill. "Do you come?"

Lumna came, for she would not be left alone here in the creeping silence of the hut, with the memories of the terrifying night to keep her company. Outside the world was gray; no color in the grass and mist still lying heavy in the valleys, the great trees on the hilltop looming like phantoms against the sky. The air was still thick with churned dust and sour with the smell of spilled ale; sickening too with a foul sweet smell that Lumna did not know. There was something strange and terrible in this wreckage of the night, some breath of awful evil and ugliness and fear.

The last of the women were fleeing down the hill into the shadows and the girl took Lumna's reluctant hand to rush her on.

"The warriors will be gone. We will miss the chariots!"

"The chariots."

She saw the girl's smile grow wolfish in the gray light.

"To see the chariots go out, that is—" She stopped, seeing Lumna's face, and turned with her toward the temple, even her rising blood-thirst faltering as she followed the younger girl's eyes.

"I told you, did I not," she whispered bravely in a few moments, "that on this night the old must be sacrificed for the young. This is what Nodens asks."

Lumna needed no hand now to pull her down the hill, glad to rush headlong from the six old men's heads spiked on poles outside the temple, blood still in their white hair, and their agonized eyes looking to the rising of the sun.

These then the gods of her people? These then the things her tribe had forgotten? These the wise and wonderful things of which the old woman spoke? She remembered the thin screaming in the night, and raced through the village as fast as she could run, just as the first warm rays of morning struck across the side of the hill onto the noise and turmoil of the departing army.

Ritually, in the long night, they had stripped their tunics and all their clothes, daubing their naked bodies with blue dye in patterns as old as the gods themselves —creatures of ugliness and terror, lashing their horses and screaming their wild, terrifying war cries. They poured like a raging sea out through the gates of the lowest palisade, followed by the foot soldiers with their swords and spears and clubs, loping along at the steady

pace which they could hold for hours. Last came the women, rushing as they had rushed from their silent huts in a stampeding mob, only Lumna and the chief's daughter a little in their rear, more silent than the rest.

She saw them hurtling down the hill ahead of her, the blue-painted howling horde, and knew them for her people. And could only think, in cold creeping terror, as she had thought earlier, of Cassilus and his awkward gestures, and Flavius, and the calm chiseled face of the tribune. These painted monsters were as strange and frightening to her as the Romans had been, except that these she knew from the beginning to be people. Her people. The Romans should be her enemies, as they were the enemies of the girl who ran bright-eyed at her side, waiting only for the moment when her spear might be allowed to find the chink in some Roman armor.

It was at this red-touched hour that Cassilus still slept, rolled like a hedgehog in his blanket, and the men of the scouting party turned over for a well-earned extra hour. They were off duty for the morning, free to ignore the flare of trumpets dying on the wind as the red marching flag rustled up over the Praetorium and the cohorts of the Seventh Legion tramped out through the open gates, followed by the rumbling wagons for the corn.

Lumna was exhausted by the time the women of the fort came to a halt, nothing in her closed life having made her ready for this long stampede across the country. She was confused and troubled by the long, ugly night, and was almost querulous when at last they stopped, without orders from anyone, yet seemingly guided by some familiar discipline. They were in a thick wood, tall pine trees closing out all but the sharpest spears of the early sun, and brown needles thick and damp under their bare feet. Faces seemed to crowd in on her from every side in the sun-shot darkness, female yet wolfish, all with the same expression of waiting, watching and listening for some signal that Lumna knew she would not understand.

"What now?" she said to the girl beside her. She longed as she had longed in the night to race away and leave them to their hungry waiting, her stomach crawling with sick knowledge that she would not like it when what they waited for should come. "What now?" she said again, and almost for something to grumble at. "There is no battle."

The girl gave her a swift look, and then glanced all around her as if to decide whether she would be noticed. Then she grabbed Lumna's hand.

"You take a chance of being slaughtered by a chariot," she said. "But come. I will show you the battle."

They wormed their way through the throng of whispering women, and Lumna wondered at what had been said about the chariot. As far as she could tell, except for the crowding urgent women, the forest held no more than the disturbed doves pouring their troubled cooing from the tall trees.

Nor could she see anything as they scrambled down-hill on the sliding carpet of the needles, the pine smell sharp under their disturbing feet, thrusting aside the bushes that grew thicker on the ground as they came lower down the slope.

"Now," said the girl. "Go quiet," and Lumna, peering, lost and bewildered, could see the sunlight growing strong where the trees ended.

They did the last stretch on their stomachs, coming out to the edge of the bushes on the level of the ground.

"Chariots?" breathed Lumna, looking to each side, waiting for the thunder and the bright slicing knives.

The girl grunted.

"Must be on the other flank." And Lumna did not understand. But she felt the assurance in the girl's voice, and lifted her head to look down the last of the hillside and see where she had been brought.

The hills here ringed a flat expanse of serene and pleasant land, warm and gold in the early sunshine with the splendor of its standing corn, ripe and waiting for the harvest.

Lumna's gasp of shock brought her almost to her feet, and the girl snatched at her angrily.

"Get down, fool. As easily killed here by a British sword as any other."

"But," Lumna said and her eyes were riveted on the small moving figures at the edges of the fields. "But— it it—"

"Romans!" The girl turned to look at her yet again as though she had no wits. "Did you think we came for anything else?"

"But," Lumna said again, hopelessly. "This is not a battle."

Below her, on the pale expanse of gently waving corn, the men of the Seventh Legion set themselves to the harvesting of the corn that was to feed them and keep them, while the damaged ships were made ready once again to set to sea. With Roman care, they marched their small team of sentries to their positions around the edges of the corn, watching the dark woods, and Lumna, knowing what they were doing, chewed her knuckles in her misery, helpless to shout at them that the enemy were already there, silent and grinning in their painted nakedness, waiting only for the moment right for killing.

"No," she whispered, as she had whispered in the night. "No," but this time the girl did not look, her face resting on her flat hands in rapt attention on the victims, a small smile on her fair face.

In her simplicity, it did not occur to Lumna that even this large number of Romans was not all of them. Cassilus would be there, she thought, and strained her eyes to see some smaller figure than the rest; Flavius the centurion, and looked to find a larger; and no doubt my lord the tribune, she thought, unconsciously using the Roman words, telling them where they should find the corn.

Helpless she stared, and could do no more than say their names in silence, tears creeping slowly and unheeded down her face. Were they not more her friends, who had given her life and disciplined kindness, than some strange tribe who shattered her with fear and ugliness and gave her nothing?

"Cassilus," she whispered again, and then from the silent sunny woods, the storm broke upon the Romans. Almost over Lumna's head, the naked tribesmen rushed screaming into the quiet fields, and from the curve of the hills the chariots thundered out, their drivers howling their bestial war cries and the whirling knives splintering the sun to fragments until blood should dim them.

She ran then almost at once, tearing herself from the grasp of the girl, who would not leave her hopes of killing to run after her. She saw only the Romans at a signal rush to the center of the fields, snatching up their arms as they ran, to form themselves into a circle with shields outside and overhead, a living wall of metal against the rushing hordes of tribesmen. So small the circles looked, against the masses pouring like a broken anthill from the dark woods. So small.

She did not wait to see it broken, nor the scattered soldiers mown down by the rushing chariots, nor the pale bright stubble of the cut corn patched and dark with blood.

She ran before all this so that she did not see, either, a dust cloud approaching from the sea, where the ever-vigilant commander had watched his cohorts going out to harvest with an anxiety he would never show them. He too had been alerted by a dust cloud, made as the chariots poured down the open stretches of the hills.

Now his small force of cavalry pounded toward the cornfields, followed by all the remaining cohorts in the camp, to rescue and bring back the Seventh Legion, who had survived beneath their tortoise shields with little loss.

Lumna saw none of this, nor the small man who had taken all Europe riding the cornfields on his little sturdy British horse, as calm as if the howling tribesmen were but a horde of flies troubling him in the summer heat of Rome. She fled at the first rush of the British, scrabbling her way back up the hill and as fast as she could run along the hill crest, toward a long blue sunlit stripe in the distance that she did not know to be the sea.

Barely she looked where she was going, stumbling and chattering to herself in misery and guilt, for these ugly men were nothing to her, and she had told them of the corn. In a moment's pride when she was full of knowing everything, proud to have been with the Romans, to know more than these fierce warriors, she had told them of the corn. Told them that the legions must have corn. They had laughed and slapped their thighs, and thrown her from the hut, and known exactly where to go.

Now Cassilus would be dead; and the great, broad, fierce centurion; and my lord the tribune with his clean hands. To Lumna, death was no longer a word that had no meaning.

She did not know how long she wandered after that, watching for settlements and avoiding them, living only on what she could scrape and pick from the harvest of the autumn hedges. She never knew how the tribesmen, excited by their small victory, rushed the Roman camp beside the sea; and Caesar fought a Roman battle, lining up his cohorts under their scarlet flags with eagles gleaming in the failing sun, so that the British flung themselves to death along the firm strong lines, fleeing in the end defeated back into their hills.

Caesar ordered six thousand slaves to be sent after him to Rome, holding forfeit the lives of the groveling chieftains if even one less should arrive. Then in the night, he broke his camp above the shingle, crowded his legions into the small number of mended ships, and set sail for Gaul, winter quarters for the legions, and the warm sweet air of Rome in triumph for himself.

Creeping thin and lonely along hedgerows draped with the crystal cobwebs of the fading summer Lumna knew of none of this, so that she did not understand what was happening to her one morning as the first frost crisped the grass, and she had begun to wonder dully if death or winter would come first. Curled asleep under a bush on the long slope of the hills to the sea, she woke to find herself being dragged out roughly by a man brandishing a long whip; no Roman but one of her own people, brown hair tangled to a wolfskin tunic and long moustaches curling in the cold, crisp air.

"Only one," he bawled, "but one is one."

Bewildered, she found herself surrounded by a vast mob of people—men, women, and children of all ages —some screaming and some weeping, some shouting with rage and many marching head down in sullen and dejected silence. Only the depth of her weak and weary sleep could have stopped the clamor from disturbing her. All of them were roped together, hand to foot, and when the man dragged her over to them, in baffled silence and half-starved stupidity, she stood dumbly among the tears and cries and lamentations and let herself be roped with all the rest.

Chapter Eight

THE spring of great Caesar's British Triumph had
come warm and early into Rome. By the day he
rode his golden chariot from the city gates to the high
temple of Jupiter on the Capitol, to offer his great
victory officially to the gods, the shadows of the cypresses were already sharp and black, and the blossom
drifting fragile on the seven hills above the winding
Tiber. The cheering Romans lined the streets in public
holiday, heaving each other aside to pelt the small, neat
figure with flowers and garlands and to cheer and stamp
and clap for the tramping legions following at his heels.
Last of all came the hostages from the conquered country, and they drew fresh breath to bawl their praises for
the mighty victory over the poor, bewildered savages
who marched last of all in his procession, roped and
chained together in their torn tunics and their skins,
small men and women with shaggy hair and high-

boned faces, staring with tired, empty eyes at all the color and the noise and glory of a Roman holiday. When the shouting was over and the streets empty, when the last spirals of perfumed smoke died above the altar on the Capitol, and Caesar had gone in purple splendor to his feasting, they would be torn from each other and bartered for by hard-faced dealers, slaves of less concern than cattle, bought by lots for grooming and selling later in the noisy markets down below the shallow staircase of the Forum.

Cassilus had not stayed to watch the last of the procession. His pleasure at being back in Rome, and his pride in his master and his commander and his marching legions grew suddenly cold and sour in his throat as he saw these shuffling lines of blank-eyed faces that looked so like his own. His cheering died into silence, and in a moment he turned and wormed his way out through the still-yelling crowd, thrusting his way through the legs of people who never even felt him go.

The arches of the great Colosseum were cool and empty. All faces were still turned toward the packed street between it and the Esquiline, and the long, curved colonnade stretched before him, striped with sunlight and the sharp black shadows of the columns.

"What matter," he said aloud, suddenly and fiercely, beating a fist against the cool stone of a great archway. "What matter. They will only be slaves, as I am, and what of that! They will be better off!"

Rebelliously he stared up toward the Forum and the waves of shouting moving on toward the Capitol, as though demanding why he should care. But somehow all that he could see against the huge red sandstone arches, and the far pillars of the Forum was a thin angry face under a fall of tangled brown hair, glaring at him across a smoking fire in a cold, wet forest, demanding whether he did not care about his people.

"I was small," he said again, defensively, exactly as he had answered her at the time. "I was small." People began to jostle him then, the crowds breaking now that the procession was past, moving on to seek the feasts laid for them in the open spaces of the city, eager for the days and nights of eating and drinking and reveling paid for by Caesar's gold. They pushed out of their noisy way without a second glance a young slave who leaned against a pillar talking to himself, his tunic bright across the breast with the house badge of the young tribune, Durus Velanius, newly back in Rome with his conquering commander.

In time, Rome settled once again to the routine turmoil of its workdays, and the shops along small, fashionable Tuscan Street, leading down to Tiber, welcomed the first great caravans of the spring padding into Rome piled with spices and rare perfumes, and silks and cottons in all the colors of their far, strange Eastern lands. Pale jade too, cool as winter Tiber to the fingers, and ivory fragile as the castles of spun sugar that graced Caesar's feasts.

"My lord, Durus!"

In a white-pillared villa high upon the Quirinal, above the roofs and courts and columns of the Forum, Durus

Velanius stood while his dresser buckled on his silver breastplate for ceremonial duty. His eyes were absent, looking out the unshuttered window down over the high walls of his peristyle to the warm, crowding city that had so held his mind through the cold years of northern service.

Absently he took his helmet from the slave, their breath ruffling the crest of scarlet feathers, unwilling to take his eyes from the pale flush of sandstone in the sun, spiked with black cypress and drifted with pale blossom and the fragile darkness of tamarisk. Rome in the young summer—and he must needs spend these years risking that he laid his bones in some benighted marsh. He sighed and turned as his wife spoke again from the doorway.

"My lord, Durus. What do you see in Rome that so takes your mind?"

Smiling, she crossed the room to him, tall, and as fair as he was dark, her sandaled feet whispering on the bright colors of the floor. He did not move, but waited for her, a small gesture sending away the two slaves.

"I spoke to you twice, my lord. What do you see?"

Durus did not answer her for a moment, looking at the fair head that reached almost as high as his own, hair banded a little more plainly than was fashionable above a serenely lovely face softened by a quirk of mischief at the corners of a wide mouth. He did not smile back at her, but took her hand in his and looked again out the wide window.

"I saw Rome," he said. "No more. But this time I

see it, and not the picture of it in my shivering mind, plastered against some frozen marsh."

She would not allow his brooding, pushing away all thoughts of the frightening years when she looked alone at Rome, and wondered in sick misery if she would look on it alone forever, her lord's bones in truth below this frozen marsh.

"And I see Rome," she said, "and have ill news for my lord!"

He could not resist smiling now at the dancing mischief that belied her words. "Ill news?"

"Ah, yes, poor Durus. The first caravans are in from India and Persia and they tell me Tuscan Street is crammed with chairs this last two days. I must go there, or the choicest of everything will be gone."

"Can you not bid the merchants come to you?"

His dark eyebrows closed a little; he did not like to think of her in the noise and clamor of the city center, forgetting all the time he was away, when she must needs be both father and mother to her small family, and strength and guidance for the whole house.

"I will take care, my lord," she murmured submissively. "The merchants keep the best always in the shops."

Now his grin was as wide as hers, and he groaned. "The best! If this is what you want, then we would be wise to prepare to move to some tenement in the valley when you come back!"

His face sobered. "Take Marcus," he said, "and do not let him leave you."

She nodded. She would want the steward in any case to pay for her purchases, as she always did.

"The boy," she asked. "Do you want him?"

"Cassilus? No, take him at your heels. Teach him a few civilized manners while we can. He is a good lad, and useful." He grinned and grimaced again. "But he cannot cook." Then his face grew a little vague, and at the same time surprised, as if his thoughts were unexpected.

"What, my lord?"

He looked at Petrona and shook his head, as one would brush away some shadow.

"I don't know why I thought of it," he said. "Unless it were all these wretches in the Triumph the other day. We took a girl, because Cassilus could not cook—I had forgotten her." He shook his head again, dismissing much the same haunting vision as had troubled Cassilus in the shadows of the Colosseum, of inimical eyes staring at him thoughtfully across a fire. "Gods, she thought we were," he said, and laughed. "Gods!" He swept his helmet underneath his arm, setting all the scarlet plumes trembling, and turned toward the door in a flash of silver greaves and breastplate, and swirling scarlet cloak.

Petrona did not ask about the gods. Other things were closer. "Did you say good-bye to the children?" she asked him, and he nodded, tenderness taking his dark face. She smiled back at him and let him go, the shared reality of home and family and happiness blotting out at once the shadowy presence of some small northern savage who had thought him to be a god.

Cassilus was bored and hot in the bright, crowded street of shops; the crush and chatter and scent of all the Roman ladies pressed on him until he longed to run the whole way down the length of Tuscan Street, though shrinking houses and then poor tenements, until he came to the pale, shining curves of Tiber, where beggar children splashed and shouted in the shallows. But he was wise and thoughtful, and he knew that, if his lord should live through Caesar's wars, then there would come a time when his days about the Empire would be done, and he would come home again to Rome for good, and need a body slave who knew more than how to skin a hare and light a fire. Or light a fire, anyway. Again he blinked at the sudden memory of that girl, as though all her roped and weary people in the Triumph had brought her back, and now she would not go away. But some day his lord might need a body slave in Rome, a good one, who had learned all Roman manners, so good a one that in the end his lord might even buy his freedom for him. Cassilus, citizen of Rome. So he dreamed behind his impassive face, standing a pace behind the steward with hands clasped correctly, taking with bent head any small bundle he was given to carry, the sun hot on his heavy hair and talk rising around him in the crowded street as thickly as the mists of Gaul.

"Boy!" The steward did not shout at him, two paces behind his mistress, but there was a snarl in his voice that told Cassilus he had spoken before. The boy jumped, and citizen Cassilus of Rome was gone.

"Sir?" Carefully he eyed the steward to see how far

he had offended. The man's hand was heavy with the whip, and his tight mouth told Cassilus that he might well know this later.

"You know, boy," he said with careful patience, that he might not offend his mistress with an angry voice, "the harness makers who work for my lord? Along the back of the Circus Maximus?"

Cassilus bent his head. He had been there with his lord, into the warm, splendid smell of leather, whole supple skins hanging like great bats along the rafters of the ceiling, and in behind the leather shop, the racks of bells and silken tassels, shining golden discs and chains, huge buckles winking in the gloom with jewels, and flaking sheets of gold laid onto the leather with fine-fingered skill to harness the most magnificent animals in Rome to the whirling chariots of the Circus.

"I know it," Cassilus said.

"Then go there. Ask them is the harness ready for my lord Durus, who has horses racing in tomorrow's Circus, and must have it. Bid them, if it is not ready, that it must must be, by this evening. Be back here," he added on a note of threat, "before my lady is done with buying."

Stupid old fool, thought Cassilus, bouncing away happily, up toward the clearer spaces of the Forum. How can I know when my lady will be done, or how can he, or even she, come to that. This was as good as half a day of holiday, for this errand could be spun out, with luck, to take him hours.

There was more air up on the wide, paved spaces of

the Forum even though the noon crowds here were as thick as down below, but the booths of the traders were spread about, so that people could move and walk between them. Idly he drifted to the far end of the Forum, where he must go down the shallow steps again to reach the narrow street leading around the far side of the Colosseum, pausing a long while to laugh at the antics of a cage of skinny apes from Ethiopia for sale from a little shriveled Roman almost as small and skinny as themselves. He whipped a pomegranate smartly from a stall while the trader bowed before a customer with the purple stripe of rank about his sleeves, spitting the red seeds and grinning at the writhings of a dandy on the barber's stool, having the hairs plucked from his chin. He caught the barber looking at him in the end, his eyes on the badge across his tunic as though he might not be unwilling to report an idle slave, so he turned and moved away rapidly, drifting down into the slave market without thinking where he walked.

It was as busy as the Forum, or as the rich and famous Tuscan Street, crammed just as they were with traders crying out their wares. But here the trade was done in people. Cassilus realized where his idle feet had taken him, and moved faster to get out the other side and across to the small street by the Circus. He did not like the market, any more than any other slave in Rome, though he himself had never stood with drooping head, chained to those rings along the wall, nor been prodded up as some poor wretch was now in front of him, onto the turntables scattering the space, where the merchandise might stand and revolve before the buyer, who could pinch its muscles or estimate its strength or beauty according to his household needs.

Most of the slaves today were from northern Europe, not draggled and dirty as they had been towed along in Caesar's triumph, but bathed and groomed now to look attractive to the customers, their long fair hair that got so much comment, left uncut.

The boy knew a moment of sick misery for these his people, but he was young, and could not take on himself the troubles of the world. They could be bought, he comforted himself, by someone as good and generous as his own lord, and what was there for pity in that? He slid on along the edges of the market, his eyes averted from those that followed him from under hair as thick and fair as was his own, from sudden cries in his own tongue, and roped hands that dragged at the iron rings in an attempt to stop him.

It was at the far end of the unhappy place that he was jostled up against them, by a large, loud-mouthed citizen with a train of slaves. Another few steps and the boy would have been out, free to rush on to the warm friendship of the harness shop, and to tell himself that he had never seen these dragging hands and desperate eyes. But the vast form of the fat Roman blocked his way, and his trail of slaves the way beyond him, so that Cassilus had to stand and wait, almost in the tied line of the slaves themselves.

"This one," the fat Roman said, and his whole great greedy face trembled in his interest. He was buying only girls. "This one. A little small, perhaps," he added critically, "and I cannot see her face."

An arm as large and hairy as the bears that danced in the villages in Gaul reached out past Cassilus' face. He could smell the rich fat with which the man's skin was anointed. He had to turn his head to save it rubbing on his face, and the fat fingers passed him and fumbled in a mass of brown hair falling over a bent head, fumbled until they found the chin and raised the face, turning it so that it was facing Cassilus two hands' breadth away.

She did not see him, nor know him, although her blue empty eyes passed over him as indifferent to his gasp of horror as they were to the fat face so close to her own and the whole seething city of Rome beyond.

"Lumna," he whispered, and dare do no more, lest he attract some attention from the buyer that would fix his mind on her. "Lumna."

She did not even seem to know her name, deep-set eyes opaque and dim, as though the monstrous changes in her world had been too much for her, and she had ceased to see it.

"H'm." The gross face creased with thought. "Not bad as these savages go. Put her up for me."

Cassilus flung up desperate hands as though he would stop them, and then let them drop.

"My lord," he cried then, and did not know that he had shouted, looking into the startled faces of the Roman and the merchant. Only Lumna did not look up; her face drooped again into the dark shelter of her hair.

"My lord!"

Now Cassilus did not wait in courtesy for the citizen to pass before the slave. He thrust his way past the clinging folds of the vast toga and through the knot of angry slaves behind, who helped him on his way with the hard heels of their sandals. In the middle of the road, below the great sandstone arches, he compelled himself to stop and think. Where was his lord, that he should not run useless over all the streets of Rome? Carefully he thought back, remembering that the clanging of the dawn bell had brought him from his sleep to the burnishing of armor, high polish on silver greave and breastplate, scarlet feathers warmed to dancing life before the fire. The barracks on the Via Tiburtina! There he would be, since he was on duty. Cassilus did not know if he breathed a murmur to the gods of Rome or Gaul before he began to run, to know himself on the right road already, though he must follow it half through Rome before he would come to the barracks itself, along the side of the Forum and out through the valley between the high rich slopes of the Viminal and the Esquiline, where the white villas of noble Rome sprawled and glittered in the sun. He did not see them, nor the shops and tenements and smaller houses that crowded closer to the road, his legs trembling and his breath tearing dry into his lungs long before he reached the pillared gateway of the barracks.

Another time he would have made some cheeky talk with the guards who crossed their lances formally to bar his way, asking them if they did not know the house badge of his lord, with whom he had come here even as a small child on his last visit home to Rome. But this time the pause for challenge was a gift to him to catch his rasping breath and tell them hoarsely who he was, padding on then desperately to the guard room, where he might only pray for help. Idle soldiers could keep him waiting till the sun was gone below the dark cypresses of the Vatican Hill—and Lumna locked inside the walls of the greasy Roman in the market.

Fortune crossed the vast paved spaces of the square in the short, steady shape of Flavius the centurion, who raised a thick, astonished eyebrow at the boy and did not speak, foursquare and silent on his feet, waiting for the heaving and the gasping to subside.

"Sir," Cassilus brought out in the end. "I must find my lord."

"Your lord has his duties. What do you want?"

"That girl." The boy's thin face was quivering with urgency, and he could not find the words to tell it fast enough. Nor did he hope much from Flavius, who would not understand, but must only get him to his lord. "That girl we had in Britain, that we took when we speared her father, and turned her loose when we came away. That girl."

Anxiously he looked into the brown face as hard and steady as the granite arches of the Circus. Flavius only nodded.

"Well."

"She is down there in the slave market, and about to be bought by a Roman, who—" Words forsook Cassilus, who did not really know himself what was wrong with the gross Roman, other than that he must not, must not get that small wild creature from the forests. Hopelessly he waved his arms in some vague gigantic shape. "He must not get her!" he shouted, and the centurion's brows came down like the grill against the circus lions.

"No business of yours," he said "Caesar took six thousand slaves. All of them will be in the markets."

"This one is my business! And," he added, and did not know why he was so certain, "if you will only tell my lord, I am sure it will be his business too."

"Why?"

Dumbly Cassilus raised hopeless hands and let them drop. "I do not know," he said at last. Then blunderingly, "But it is the kind of thing that would trouble my lord that one who served him even for a little should go to the house of such a man."

A long time the centurion looked at him, his great barrel chest rising and falling underneath his leather tunic, as though he needed time to understand the mind he loved, but that did not work as did his own.

"It could be as you say," he said in the end. "And I could be blamed to let such foolishness past, when you have told me. I will see my lord."

In the shadow of the guardhouse, Cassilus stood and calmed his desperate breath, looking away down the last stretches of the Via Tiburtina to where the hills flattened into the green country of small farms beyond the city. But he saw only the sun-shot forest up above the lake, and deep blue eyes watching him whenever he turned to see if the girl was following. Suddenly he felt filled with an excitement he did not understand; the sun more hot, and the warm scents of spring as sudden on the air as though they had just arrived for him alone. He turned and grinned broadly back at the pale, cypressed city piled haphazard on its seven hills. Now he would show her Rome.

He was still grinning when Flavius came back at the same steady pace, brown face still impassive.

"You were right about your lord," he said, as though never would he understand the foolishness of his superiors. "He sent you this to take at once to his steward." Cassilus snatched eagerly at the tablet. "It is instructions to buy the girl if she is still there, and if not, to find out the buyer from the merchant and offer him whatever he may want to part with her."

Chapter Nine

I T was some while before the sightless look left Lumna's
eyes, before she understood with amazement and
dawning happiness that she was in the household of the
young officer with the long, clean fingers, who had so
long ago refused to kill her. Now it seemed he had refused to allow her to be sold into unhappiness or cruelty,
taking her instead into service in his own house, where
the lady Petrona settled her among the women waiting
on her children.

It was to Cassilus that she began first of all to speak,
even while she still stood quivering and silent before the
kindness of her mistress, unable yet to reshape her understanding of her world. First she talked of the long,
bitter winter of her journey to Rome, crouched beside
him in a corner of the back courtyard where the slaves
were free to walk and sit in their small moments of rest.

"I saw them," she said to him suddenly one evening,

when he had despaired of ever getting her to speak, her blue eyes turning on him more alive and urgent than he had ever seen them. "I saw them."

"Saw what?" Cassilus was gentle, with some blind understanding that she must not be hurried. The passage from the silent lake to Rome had been too drastic, and now her mind must follow and catch up.

"I saw the great stones," she said, and her urgent eyes grew distant. "In Gaul, they said it was, where we walked and walked and walked, and the frost came and bound the ground under our feet. And snow fell and many died of cold, and still we walked, until we came to another sea." She stopped, as though weary all over again with the terrible prisoners' march down through winter Gaul to the slave ships on the Middle Sea. "I saw them then," she went on. "The great stones, eight times higher than a man, marching the hilltops like the legions themselves."

Now without thought she used all the words that in the end of summer had been a mystery to her. She knew now all about the legions and the commander and the sea and ships.

Cassilus groped back in his mind to their talks across the embers in the forest, to some thing he had told her, when she asked from where the Romans came. From great plains, she had asked him, with tall stones that trapped the sun?

"The stones of the gods?" he said to her hopefully, trying to keep her talking. The sun moved around and struck brown rich lights from her hair that was now clean and shining, and by her feet a small lizard scuttled from a crack. She was too occupied to notice it.

"The old woman told me," she went on, now almost as though she was repeating a lesson that she had found to her amazement to be wrong. "She told me of the world beyond the lake, and of the great stones and the gods, but I found the gods, and the people, of my old woman's world."

Abruptly she stopped.

"Well," he said, afraid to say too much lest she should stop. This must all have happened after they turned her toward her home.

"Why," she demanded suddenly, turning to him, as though it had but just come clearly to her mind. "Why were you not killed in the cornfield with all the others? And why was my lord not killed, and the square man, that I have seen here walking with him in the—peristyle?" Quickly she was learning all the names of this beautiful new world in which she found herself.

"Killed, in the cornfield?" Again Cassilus thought back. "With the Seventh Legion? I was not there, nor was my lord nor the centurion. How were you there to know of it?"

She stared down at her clean sandaled feet. Clearly she had been wrong again. Not even all the Romans in the cornfield had been *all* the Romans. And how many more must there be in Rome.

"My people have no chance," she said, apparently without sense.

Cassilus was patient. So much she was saying made

no sense. There seemed much she had to sort and settle.

"Tell me," he said, "all that happened to you after we left you."

A little she spoke, of wandering the woods and losing all contact with him and the Romans, and then of coming in the morning to the girls in the oak grove and the fort on the hill. Here she grew silent, her tunic twisting madly in her fingers, with no words to go on. Cassilus watched her, puzzled, and then she turned and looked at him as though begging desperately for some help, only to turn away again, with slow tears forcing themselves from under her closed lids, and her breath coming in a long, desperate effort not to weep.

"I told them," she said in the end, and every word held the long winter's burden of her guilt toward those who had been good to her. "I told them about the corn-fields and I thought you were dead, and my lord and the square man, and all the other Romans too."

"You told them about the cornfields?" Still he did not quite understand. Certainly the Seventh Legion had been ambushed, but what could she know of it? The commander had expected it in any case, and small harm was done; indeed, it made the tribes foolhardy for their final defeat. He said no more than to tell her gently to tell him all the tale, and she gulped her tears and breathed awhile in the warm silence. No sound in the rich declining sun but the soft laughter of three Ethiopian boys who lounged across the courtyard, one strumming softly on some strange sad instrument with strings.

She told him everything then, except about the dark,

wild night of fear and evil and horror, and the old severed heads along the spikes in the dawn, and in the end she looked at him in amazement that he should laugh. There was a look of tenderness beyond his years on his long, fair face as he stared at her and shook his head.

"All the long winter of the march down Gaul," he said, and began to laugh again, "you have told yourself that you destroyed the Roman army."

Miserably she nodded. It was not so easy to shake off the guilt.

Suddenly he sobered, looking at her curiously.

"But why should you mind?" he asked her. "The British are your people. You told me so."

Her head dropped, and her face was hidden by the shining fall of long brown hair. How could she tell him of her hopeless confusion about believing in her people until she saw those fearful heads up on the spikes? How could she tell him that he himself had a lot to do with it, that she thought she had killed him, and how she had been shaken and confused by something as foolish as the long, clean fingers of their lord?

"In the forest," she said, and said only a small part of it. "The Romans were good to me."

He let it go at that, and began to grin again, telling her how Caesar had foreseen there might be an attack on the cornfields, and had got his men safely back with small losses, then how the Britons had grown too sure of themselves and attacked the camp, being completely routed and defeated.

"That is why you are here," he said, and she looked at him questioningly.

"Caesar demanded hostages, and slaves at pain of their death."

"Hostages?"

"When he conquers a country, he demands thousands of its people to come to Rome as slaves. He holds the lives of chieftains hostage that they shall be sent. A sort of price they must pay for having fought against him."

"Caesar has conquered Britain now?"

"Not yet, but he will, and then it will be as Rome."

He did not notice the sudden dark preoccupation of her eyes.

"Anyway," he said then, "even if you did not kill me in the cornfield, you got yourself to Rome, and that is what I wanted from the beginning. Now you will know what I was talking of in the forest."

She looked all around her slowly, and even in this plain court at the back of the villa for the slaves, the peace and beauty of Rome was apparent in the tall pillars and flowers breaking into tender color along the green roof tiles, the lambent sky flushing into the first purple of exquisite dusk. Then she turned back and smiled at him, a smile of pure pleasure that transformed her gloomy and hostile little face, so that he stared at her in surprise and had found no words when the cool clangor of the bell of hours sounded through the house.

Both jumped immediately, and across the paved court the Ethiopians dropped their music and padded off on great soft feet, all of them away before the clack of Marcus' sandals disturbed the colonnade, and his sharp eyes raked the court for idle slaves.

Lumna was intelligent, and cleared of her burden of guilt and ugliness and the weariness of her long, terrible journey, she began rapidly to learn of life as it was lived in Rome, to watch and listen, and take every opportunity to understand this world more calm and beautiful than any that her people had ever dreamed. Even the people, she thought soberly, of the wider world of which the old woman talked. Here was the wider world.

She valued every hour of every day, from the dawn bell that dragged her from her sleep into the morning rush of cleaning with all the other slaves, a turmoil of buckets and ladders and poles and sponges and brooms that must all be done and cleared away before the shutters were opened on the plain, beautiful bedrooms of Durus and the lady Petrona, letting in the flooding sun of the Roman spring and all the confused hum of the city center in the middle of the hills.

She would help to dress the two small, laughing girls and the solemn little boy with his black hair cropped on his round head, and his father's steady eyes. In the bright morning, watched by the older women in charge of the children, she would play with them in the sheltered spaces of the peristyle, the air already sweet with the scent of thyme and drifts of white narcissi, the first roses budding on the loggias. She tumbled with them on the short green turf, and took off her sandals to feel the sun warm under her feet as they chased her through the colonnades. She tossed their colored balls and helped the little girls to dress their dolls, filled his small cart with sand for the solemn tiny boy and helped him to pull it where his games demanded. She helped them feed the two big, gentle dogs that shared their days, taking their food already prepared from yet another slave, smiling her contentment at the children's tall, soft-spoken mother, who watched her and thought about her, and in the end asked Durus why these people from Britain were always spoken of as savages.

"Savages?" Durus shook his head, his mind still full of Caesar's plans for the summer. "They *are* savages."

Petrona shook her fair head. "This one thinks, and she is as gentle with our children as myself."

"Which one?" Durus had forgotten, as soon as the arrangements to protect her had been made.

"The one you bought for me, dearest. She was with you, you said, in Britain."

"Ah, yes." The long, thin face relaxed into the smile that so changed it. "Ah, yes, the little one who thought I was a god. She knows better now, no doubt." Then his face sobered, as though he looked back again at Lumna in the forest. "You could be right in saying that she thinks, that little one. She thought a lot about us."

When a little time had passed, and Lumna's training had progressed under the fierce eye of the mistress of the slaves, she was allowed to wait on the lady Petrona as she moved about the city, following her through the long, bright afternoons of Roman spring as she picked and drifted along the gay shops of Tuscan Street, or visited her friends in their white-walled villas on the hills above the city. Her eyes missed nothing of all the wonders Cassilus had spoken of so long ago half across the world, and she had not understood him. Now she knew the meaning of streets paved wide enough for seven chariots, and huge buildings made of stone piled upon itself, and white houses gleaming in the sunshine, where her mistress was welcomed through heavy doors with great pillars of carved marble. She stood beside her in an atrium as large as all her father's island, bright with cushions and adrift with flowers, the sound of falling water a background to the soft cooing of the pigeons strutting on the colored floor.

It was all as large as he had said, and just as wonderful, but it was something else. Something that made her catch her breath and struggle with the tears pricking at her eyes as she saw this Roman city, and then remember that her people lived as she had lived, in their mud huts of chilly damp, along the lake shore. She did not know what it was that so upset her; she had not yet learned the word for beauty.

The evenings she loved best of all, when about the fourteenth hour, the family would gather for its evening meal, Durus Velanius off duty from the barracks and her lady back from the afternoon of visits. Lumna herself would be bidden to stand behind the children to help them with their food, but first of all all slaves were summoned to the long pillared room, where daily sacrifice was made to the gods who cared for homes and families such as this. No bloody ritual of severed heads, but a gentle ceremony with prayers by the young father of the household, bending his dark head over mild libations of milk and honey, begging the blessing of his household gods on his home and all who lived in it, his tranquil wife and his little daughters and the small, sleepy son who fidgeted behind him on the marble floor.

There would be fine foods then, and wines that glowed pale and splendid in clear crystal goblets, pitchers of milk for the small ones, piled fruit from the blossoming orchards beyond the city walls, and the sweet nutty smell of new-baked bread, waiting for the cutting of great golden cheeses or the spread of yellow honey, sweet from the herbs of the northern hills. Flowers glowed in garlands along the center of the marble table and the sun itself would be flooding in, rose-red from the west, across the shining curves of Tiber, mixing with the lamplight and the acrid yellow of new kindled torches, falling in soft pools across the checkered floor.

The room would know laughter then about the long table, and soft voices, and the father would ask the little ones to tell him of their day. At the meal's end, the girls would reach for their ribboned lutes and play for him, with anxious mouths and short inexpert fingers, while the small boy lolled and dozed against his knee, smiling and eating sugared grapes. From her silent corner Lumna watched, even as she might peer into the dwellings of the gods, remembering the mud hut and the screaming children, and the harsh-voiced mother almost with bewilderment, as though they had belonged to someone else.

The lady Petrona herself had taught her to sew, hearing from the mistress of the slaves of her astonishingly quick and clever fingers.

"Did you never sew before?" she asked her, as she watched the girl's grave delight in color and pattern creeping into life beneath her flying needle.

Lumna could hardly bring herself to stop, so great was her pleasure in the skill she never knew she had. For a fleeting moment she saw the picture of her mother's stubby fingers wrestling with a crude bone needle to join two wolfskins against the winter; then she looked down at the color in her lap, and answered, as every question from mistress to slave must at once be answered.

Petrona had brought her in to her own small room, opening on to the flower-filled peristyle, partly since the mistress had been startled by her skill, but mostly out of curiosity. Savages, they called them, all these people from the cold northern corners of the Empire, but Durus had had the boy Cassilus some years now, and he grew more Roman every day, nor did this blue-eyed creature seem anything but docile and nimble in her fingers.

"Are you happy in Rome?" she asked her pleasantly, having no idea, the gods knew, of what her home and her country were really like or, if she found it all completely strange. "Is there anything you would like to ask me?"

Lumna looked up, full demanding gaze of the deep-set eyes. She could ask questions of her lady until the sun was gone, but had never dared. The first rule taught to a slave was silence unless asked to speak. Also, although her quick ear had taught her rapidly to know what was said around her, she found it still difficult to talk. One thing was uppermost in her mind.

"My lady," she said, and spoke haltingly, troubled by her lack of speech, and her real horror with her own people, "all the gods in Rome seem to be gentle ones."

Petrona creased her fair eyebrows. What did the child mean?

"Gentle ones?"

"When my lord prays before the evening meal, he offers only meal and milk and honey and harmless things like that. Is it always so in Rome? Never," she paused and thrust away the sick memory that made her speak. "Never—humans?"

Petrona grimaced gently at the thought of a messy human sacrifice on her cool marble floor, and how it would outrage her fastidious Durus, but the child for some reason was deadly serious, looking at her with some desperate expression in her eyes. Carefully she thought, to give her honest answer. On the whole it was right that there was no human sacrifice. There was talk and whispering about the goings on of the priests of Mithras and Cybele, and some more dark religions of the East, but these were truly no concern of Rome.

"No," she said firmly. "No. In big ceremonies in the temples, they may sacrifice a bull or a sheep, but that is all. Why do you ask?"

"Never humans?" Lumna repeated, and did not

answer the question. "What if you sacrifice to the god of war?"

"It is the same. You can get the boy Cassilus to take you to the temple of Mars, the god of war, and you can see for yourself. There are many sacrifices there at the moment."

Full of all her own confusion of thoughts, Lumna did not see how her lady's face grew sick and shadowed on her last words, or how she bent her head with sudden silence over her work frame, and did not speak again until they both looked up at the clicking latch of the heavy door leading from the house out to the peristyle.

"Ah," cried Petrona. "Here is my lord."

Sadness was flown, even at the sight of him, no longer a ceremonial soldier, but dressed in the bemetaled leather in which Lumna had first seen him, so far from Rome and from this scented garden. Dressed again as a soldier who made ready to go to war. But Lumna's mind had so much to work on that still she did not see this, and in silence she watched him, even as his lady did, her long mouth curved in tenderness. He came slowly across the long, beautiful spaces of the peristyle, and here he stopped to lift the budding roses and mark how they did, there he paused to pick a bunch of thyme and crush it in his fingers, all the suns of previous summers pouring from its crumpled sweetness. In the end, he leaned with hands spread out on the low marble wall, where the garden looked out over Rome. A long time he stood there, and in the end turned a little toward them so that they could see his face.

"Oh, my lord," his lady breathed, and her voice was the echo of the deadly grief of his expression as he looked at his beloved city, thinking himself to be alone. "Oh, my lord."

She was on her feet to run to him almost before she spoke, all the bright silks tumbled to the floor at her feet, but before she reached him, the little girls came rushing through the archway at the far end of the garden, shouting for their father, with the small black-haired brother trotting along behind.

When Lumna looked up from gathering the spilled silks, all grief was fled, nor did she understand what he was grieving for. His small son sitting on his shoulders and pulling at his helmet, he teased and ruffled the two girls, his wife leaning on the parapet in the sun, looking at them all with sweet affectionate eyes.

A few moments she stared, afraid of being caught looking at them.

"They are but people," she said to herself, and did not remember that she had said just this to Cassilus, in the forests above the sea, with the wind rising in the trees. "They are but people, but they are not like us."

She told all this to Cassilus, in one of their snatched moments in between their tasks. It was raining, soft, endless, determined rain that poured from a gray sky and blotted out the seven hills as though Rome lay upon a plain. They sat within the shelter of the colonnade, and watched the water bouncing from the paved floor.

"You make the Romans seem a soft, foolish lot," cried Cassilus, almost angry. "How do you think they have conquered half the world? And will get the other half?"

Lumna stared at her fingers, trying to tell him what she meant.

"They can be very cruel," he went on before she could. "When we have public holiday, I will ask Marcus to let me take you to the Circus. Slaves can go. Then you will see that they can be cruel."

"The Circus?"

He told her bluntly of all the most bestial of the Circus entertainments; the gladiators fighting lions with their bare hands, the great Ethiopians greased from head to foot, left to wrestle through to death, the combats to death between one man with a spear and one a sword.

"Death is their fun, I tell you," he cried, anxious to shock her, and her eyebrows creased together.

"Yes," she said, and struggled desperately to some understanding of what she thought. "But they know they like it." Sickness rose up in her again at the memory of some dreadfulness and evil in the dark night on the hill fort. "They do not enjoy it," she cried, remembering the howling and the yelling through the long night, "and then pretend it is all for the gods."

He looked at her amazed, his small savage that he had himself taken from her lake dwelling hardly able to speak a word.

"That is why," she went on somberly, thinking of the clean, hard lines of the face of Durus Velanius, that was yet the most gentle she had ever seen, also of the square Flavius, goodnatured and friendly, who would yet have killed her when he thought it his duty. "That is why the Romans fight so well. They know about themselves. My people will not stand a chance when this Caesar chooses to go back again."

Cassilus looked suddenly eager and about to speak, but she went on.

"I suppose when he has defeated them, he will build roads for them, and cities like Rome, and baths and stone houses, and all the things the Romans have, and they will be far better off."

"Of course," Cassilus said, as though abandoning what he was going to say, eyebrows still up in his fair fringe as he looked at her.

"It would be easier for them surely if they did not fight, but made the Romans welcome, and learned all these things from them."

Cassilus did his best, scratching his thick hair and wondering what in thunder she was talking of.

"Ah," he said, and thought it to end the conversation. "But how would they know to do this?"

Lumna stared a long time at the rain, and there was no sound but the laughter and occasional cries of a party of slaves playing dice along the colonnade. Finally she turned on him eyes as blue and clear as the Middle Sea.

"Someone could tell them," she said, and slipped away, leaving him staring after her, stopped from laughing by some fear of this new Lumna, as a magician might be terrified at the small spirit he has conjured up when it swells suddenly to twice his size.

Chapter Ten

I N the weeks that followed it seemed as though Lumna shed all the guilt and memories of horror that had dogged her through the winter of her capture. She now allowed herself to slide with drifting content into the ways of her new household and of life in Rome. She asked no more questions, but only watched and listened and absorbed everything she saw and heard, as though for some reason her time for learning it was short.

Cassilus, watching her, was amazed to see her sliding so happily into the life she had once despised, her own people forgotten, or so it seemed, and the aggressive little savage of the forest now turning rapidly into one of the neatest and most quick-fingered slaves who waited on the lady Petrona.

"I tell you," he said to her one day, "I think you are even growing like a Roman! You are taller than that day I plucked you from the market!"

She only smiled. She smiled now more easily, changing the whole look of her narrow face that had once been sullen and aggressive, and often as he was passing through the colonnades of the house, he would hear her laughing with the children.

"And you laugh," he went on then almost accusingly. "You never laughed in the forest!" It was almost as though he resented the neat, smooth-haired girl who sat beside him in the sun, skillfully tossing five stones and catching them in ones and twos along the back of her brown hand. Resented that he had little more to teach her, that almost overnight she had become more Roman than himself. Some contrary instinct made him want to taunt her with the change, and ask her what she thought now about her own people, and did she want to go back to her swamp. But there was a strange firmness in the narrow face that made him hold his tongue, almost for some reason a little bit afraid of her.

"You are happy in Rome." It was almost an accusation that he leveled at her, he who once could not wait to get her here, jealous now that she seemed even more at home than he did, in so short a time.

"You must not think," he said, waving a general hand all around the villa, "that only this is Rome. There are poor people in Rome too. Not every Roman lives like this."

Lumna stopped tossing her stones and frowned at him, pushing back her brown hair in the gesture that had not changed at all, with all the changes that had come to her. She did not understand why he seemed to be angry with her, and she answered him quietly. "I know."

"How?" This exasperating girl could be told nothing.

"My lady gave me a few hours of holiday one day, and the square man called Flavius took me to his home. He was in the kitchens, and when I said I did not know what to do with my holiday, he took me home."

"Flavius is not poor. He is a centurion."

Patiently she answered again. "He is not like my lord. Down in the valley he has a small house, with three rooms, and no walls about it such as this. But there are separate places for living and for sleeping and for preparing food. They have no children, and it is very clean."

She fiddled with the smooth stones in her hands, and the withdrawn look was on her face again.

"I walked with him through the poorer streets, and I tell you that not the poorest man in Rome lives as my people do beside the lake."

She smiled suddenly, small teeth white in a face that was brown and glowing from the Roman sun.

"Flavius is kind. He would not kill me now."

"Hm," said the boy, and suddenly hated even Flavius, who seemed to have had more to do with this new Lumna than he had.

She was playing with her pebbles again, clattering them to the sun-warmed stones.

"Listen," he said, "in three days there is a public holiday, to see the legions march through Rome. Will you let me take you to watch them?"

168

She smoothed the skirt of her tunic, pale green as the young leaves that unfolded on the almonds now that the pink surge of their blossoming was over.

"I will have to ask my lady," she said, "and the mistress of the slaves."

"Well ask them," Cassilus cried, truculent. Where was the little savage who had run so obediently at his heels in Britain? Could she not show a little more enthuiasm? She stood up then and collected her pebbles, the green skirt blowing a little in the gentle wind. All of Petrona's slaves wore this shade of tender green, but the bewildered Cassilus could not understand why it was that he saw it only on this obstinate girl.

He could not know that of all the things that Rome had taught her, the most important to Lumna was that she had learned she was a girl. Learned to know what it was she had so longed for in the bleak, cold hut beside the lake. It was not a wider world in truth, but was all the things she had now here in Rome, light and quietness and soft colors, clean hair and gentle voices and an ordered life. All the things that allowed her to remember she was a girl, even if she was a slave, and not a savage in a wolfskin, fighting with all the rest of her tribe that she might live until another spring.

"I will ask them," she said now, and then the whisper of her sandals was gone along the colonnade, and Cassilus strugged and made for the stables where he must polish harness for his lord. Not the bright gilded harness of the Circus, but the hard plain leather of horses that must go to war, leather that would have to last through cold and damp in a climate far from the warm easy sun of Rome.

He knew well where he was going, and before very long. All Rome knew of it, even before the parade of the legions in the streets, to tell the citizens of another expedition in their name, to add to the glory of both Rome and Caesar. But until this day, when it became the public news of Rome, the army did not speak of it, nor did their slaves. Durus Velanius would come home daily in his leather uniform with smiling talk of how he and his Petrona would spend their summer in the Alban Hills. Or perhaps take themselves a villa beside the green warm seas that lapped Capri? And Petrona would smile and listen and talk as happily as he; only her secret heart would gnaw at her with the certain knowledge that she and her children alone would gather honey in the hills, or bathe in the green shallows along the snow white sand.

Only Lumna, concerned and occupied with all she had to learn and master in this strange place, inward-looking in all her fresh discoveries about herself, was not aware of what was going on. She knew that Julius Caesar planned to go again to complete the conquest of her country, but she had no thought that it would be yet. So absorbed with all that had happened to herself, it never occurred to her that there had been time for the commander to prepare an army and plan a new campaign, that the blossoming summer that brought her so much pleasure was to him no more than the rearing of the harvest to feed his troops when he brought them back to Britain toward the autumn. The cavalry and some of the legions had remained in Gaul in winter quarters. Only enough of them had come home to make a Roman Triumph for their leader, who was already back on the sea coast facing Britain, brooding on the lessons he had learned last year, and determined this time that he would suffer nothing from his enemy, the sea.

Lumna had been unaware of any atmosphere, indifferent to the marching soldiers in the streets, and the endless scream of trumpets from the barracks here and there about the city, where the legions drilled and mustered, cursing as they gathered their equipment for another expedition to that benighted swamp. She was smiling and cheerful as she met Cassilus outside the plain wooden door in the back wall of the villa, which was for the use of slaves. Every servant in the house was pouring gaily out for their day's holiday, when the people of the house would care for themselves, with the help of those too old or too devoted ever to leave them, even for a day.

"Where will we go? Where will we see best?"

She was almost dancing along, head up to the sun, and the wind that whipped her green skirts was warm and heady with the smell of musk and tamarisk and the sweet perfume of the roses that fell in pink and crimson showers above the garden walls. The road of beaten earth sloped down toward the green roofs of the Forum, down to where the paved streets began near the center of the city. From all the seven hills a small haze of dust held Rome, from the feet of its people pouring down the hills on just such roads and in from all the small farms beyond the city, and the wide pastures of the Campagna, to do honor to great Caesar's legions before they sailed to bring more honor home to Rome.

"Along beside the Colosseum." he answered. "Then if it gets too hot, we can move back under the arches."

She nodded and hurried on a little through the steadily growing crowd that poured downhill toward the city. Secretly he was surprised at her; he would have thought it would have angered her, and started one of her stubborn fits, to be asked to go and cheer the legions that were off to conquer Britain. He would have expected her to have refused to go, to stay at home in sullen silence, instead of joining gaily in the holiday. Shrugging, he gave it up, and yielded himself to the day and to the cheerful crowd tramping along between the rows of hustlers selling sherbet cups and sugared pomegranates, and balls of paper streamers for throwing at the grinning troops.

It was almost over before she asked the question that started all the trouble. Until then she had been content to stand where he held her balanced on the lowest plinth of a sandstone pillar, a head above the crowd where she could see the rank on rank of swinging kilts go by, and leather helmets rising and falling in rows as neat as if they had been joined with rope. She knew now the meaning of the great gold eagles carried before each cohort of the legions, the rank of a man who wore a flaring scarlet cloak, and of one whose cloak fell purple to the high tops of his laced leather boots. She knew now about the legions. And about Romans. They were no longer a handful of terrifying strangers in her forest, so strange and mystical that she had thought them gods. With the memory, she found it so foolish that she smiled suddenly down at Cassilus, steadying herself with a hand on his hair. It was agony, pulling on the roots, and dragging his scalp, but he would have gladly stayed there until the last soldier was passed, filled with astonishment and confused delight at that warm, sudden smile. Then she shifted her hand about his shoulder and leaned down to him as though the thought had just occurred to her, brown hair and fair mingling on his shoulder.

"Where are they going?" she asked almost idly. "Do they go to war?"

He looked up at her appalled.

"You did not know?"

In silence she stared back at him, and then slowly shook her head, turning then to look at the soldiers marching through the canyon of applause with very different eyes. There was no need for him to tell her now where they were going. Why had she not thought of it for herself?

"I thought—I thought," she said to him, bewildered. "Some time, but not yet."

It seemed so short a time since she had crouched below the bushes at the edge of the cornfield, the year shrunk by all the immense things that had happened to her. It had not occurred to her that there had been

time for Caesar to go there again, with another army, half across the world, or so it seemed.

"It is so far," she said, voicing only half her thoughts.

"No," said Cassilus. "It took long the way you came, because no one cared if you got here or not. But Caesar wants his legions, and they will get there quickly."

Once more she looked at the men and listened to the dull thump of their heavy boots, growing hollow now as the end of the last column wound its way around the

curve of the Circus. Almost dazed, she stared at them, driven to come at once to decisions that were only half formed in her mind. With a stunned, bewildered air she gave her two hands to Cassilus to lift her down off the pillar. Holding them a second longer than he needed, like some precious captive bird, he recalled her desperate independence in the screaming wind-torn forest, when, blue with cold, she would not share his Roman cloak. Was it Rome alone that had so gentled her?

She moved out of the crowd almost as though she did not see them, and when she sat down, drawing aside the almond skirts to leave room for him, on one of the red steps of the Circus, her first words were not of herself.

"Our lord, Durus?"

Cassilus was nonchalant.

"Oh, yes, he must go."

"The lady Petrona," she said then, and it was not a question, but a statement of pity, of understanding for grief and loneliness that the small savage from the lake would never have known.

Again, Cassilus was airy, waiting for her to come to the one person whose absence he really wanted to discuss.

"The lady Petrona is used to it," said Cassilus, and then at last she came to it.

"And you," she said, "will go with my lord." Faintly she grinned and glanced at him sideways. "To skin his hares and cook for him."

People were scattering now the parade was over,

tramping over their feet and stumbling on their knees, brushing their faces with skirts and togas, and Cassilus waited irritably and hopelessly for her to say something about missing him, before he would have to say it for himself.

What she did say left him sitting with his mouth wide open, staring at her and taking no heed of the passing, pressing people, until he found himself enmeshed in the blue gauze of a lady's scarf, limp and soft and clinging to his face. Furiously he clawed it from his eyes and faced her.

"You will do *what?*" he asked her.

Calmly she looked at him, as if to ask what all the uproar was about.

"I said I will go with you. Is it not my country?"

Almost speechless, he gestured at the springing arches far above their heads, vaguely around him at the rising hills of Rome, and then at the girl herself and her floating dress of almond green.

"All this," he cried, amazed, "and you would go back to being a savage by a stagnant lake?"

Tears of anger sprang into her eyes.

"Yes," she shouted at him, "yes, I would go back to the stagnant lake but not to be a savage."

"What else!"

Desperately she ground her hands together, one inside the other, her head bowed above them, knowing the battle she was going to have to fight.

"I told you," she said, with careful patience, oblivious now of the floating cloaks and skirts and togas brushing on her face. "I told you," she said, pushing them aside and almost their owners with them, "that someone should go back and tell my people of the Romans, that they were but people like themselves, but knowing so much more. If they would not fight, but only listen, then they would have life itself, and with it all these things the Romans have. Someone must tell them."

"You are a fool."

In his anxiety for her, he was brutal, rude, but her anger was calming and did not flare again.

"I am not. I am a chief's daughter. I could tell my people, and send them on to tell others, and spread the word that these Romans have so much to teach."

He was still furious and afraid. "These savages could not learn!"

Quietly she dropped her head, and now the crowds were thinning so that he could see the lowered lids and the small tightening of the mouth as she gulped back her anger.

"I have learned," she said to him, lifting her head, her eyes blue and dark and determined. In his shame he did not know where to look, nor could he find the words to tell her that he did not care one jot about her people; he cared only that she should not go back into the middle of a land at war, for this time Caesar did not mean to stop at the coast. He did not want her in danger, among violence and death; he himself must go with his lord, but he had pictured her staying in calm and safety with the lady Petrona, where he would find her when he came back. But he was too young and blundering to tell her this, and could only try another track, his high, fair cheekbones flushed with distress.

"You will never find your people."

"You will help me."

"I?" Now plain horror took his voice, that not only would she go, but try to take him with her in this mad-brained expedition. "What would your people want with me?"

Once more she looked at him, as if she read his mind, and once more he looked away in shame.

"I do not want you with me," she said contemptuously, "only that you find the way for me."

He did not know what was coming next, and merely looked at her determined face in resigned silence.

"You go almost daily to the barracks with my lord?"

He nodded.

"Then you will find the map he made of my country for the corn."

She must have taken total leave of all her senses.

"I could not take that from the legions. It is their life to know where they can find food and drink!"

"You need not take it." A small, derisive hand swept at all his objections. "You need only look at it, and tell me how the land lies, high or low, and what water between the lake and the sea, and where to place the sun. I will find it."

He had nothing to say. She had an answer ready for it all. She must have thought of this for weeks and weeks, almost since she came into the house of Durus Velanius.

"Well," she said tartly, "can you not read a map? Surely if I have learned to make a colored bird fly beneath my needle, you, the tribune's body slave, have picked up how to read a map."

This rallied him again, turning on her furiously.

"Of course I know how to read a map!"

"Then that is good. I will know how to find the way. Remember," she said bitterly, "I am a savage."

There were all sorts of entertainment in the public parks, but neither of them had any heart for them, and so trailed back up the hill toward the villa in the hot, bright afternoon, with the cicadas rattling in the grass along the roadsides and small harebells trembling in the wind.

It was only when they were in the shadow of the high white walls themselves that she turned and looked back down over Rome—white walls and brown and pink, sleeping in the heat all up and down the hills with a faint gleam of far Tiber in the sun, laden with roses in its gardens and the tall fragrant stems of lilies, freesia and thyme and the feathery fronds of tamarisk. Appalled he watched her, seeing the blue eyes fill with tears as she stared across the city, lids falling over them too late to stop them creeping painfully down her cheeks. She did not lift a hand to wipe them off, and there was something that tore his young heart to see her so, his small savage with so much dignity, standing there in her green gown, weeping, so it seemed, for Rome.

With infinite courage he took her hand in his. She did not snatch it from him, but he did not dare to speak, and in the end she opened drowned blue eyes and turned to him.

"I know I was foolish," she said. "But I did not think it would be so soon."

They sat down then, in quietness, on the dry grass high above the city, in the shadow of the tribune's walls. He listened patiently to all her plans, and did not tell her again she was a fool. He knew that no matter what madness she might ask him in the way of help, he would be unable to refuse.

Chapter Eleven

Now that she was aware of what was happening, Lumna realized the preparations for the expedition to Britain were on every side of her in Rome. Now she heard the endless trumpet calls from the barracks, and the nailed boots along the paved roads of the city, the rolling of wagons through the hours of darkness, rising like thunder from the valleys as supplies were taken to the ships lying ready at the port beyond the marshes. She did not urge Cassilus, but every time she passed him in the house, with properly folded hands and bent head, her eyes would flick a question to which he could only shake his head.

It was the third day after their talk that he at last found himself alone in the room which his lord shared as an officer with three other young Roman nobles of the same rank, every soldier in the barracks except those on sentry out on the parade ground, having their equipment inspected for the expedition.

"Guard the place, Cassilus," his lord had said, as he handed him his helmet. "I would seem to be the only one with a body slave today. Bid anybody that comes to wait, though they may well wait a while."

Cassilus listened to the hard clack of his nailed boots along the tiled corridor, others joining them in a crescendo of noise that slowly died away, changing then to the flare of trumpets and the shouting of commands, the crash of a thousand turning feet away below the windows in the hot sunshine. Silence held the room, and when he peered outside, no one stirred in the long passage, checkered in sun and shadow by the square colonnading along its open side.

He had too often waited on his lord here not to know where the maps and charts were kept, too often watched them hang one or other on the wall and talk about it, for him not to understand how he must read it. The heavy lid of the map chest creaked a little as he lifted it, and he looked fearfully behind him at the leather curtain of the door, and then down into the ordered rows of parchment rolls, each one tied with tape and labeled on its scarlet seals for what it was.

Carefully he began to search, disturbing as little as he could, glancing every so often out the window to where the Praetor moved slowly down the ranks of small brown figures, each with his pile of belongings at his feet. He could not find the maps of Britain. Sweat began to break along his forehead, and at a distant footstep he slammed the chest and shot back to his place against the wall behind his master's table. But no one came, and silence fell again, no sudden loud commands, no trumpets flaring for dismiss. Wiping his hands along the colored front of his tunic, he breathed deeply to try and steady the sick thudding of his heart. She had not stopped to ask, this girl, what would be the penalties for a slave found stealing the military secrets of the Republic? What would happen to him if it were not his lord who walked in at the moment he was searching in the chest? Even if it were his lord?

Suddenly fear fell from him, like the loosening of a screw about his head, his hands fell to his sides and he began to laugh, stifling it at once in the silence. He was as big a fool as was the girl. Rifling in the store chest for the maps of an expedition that was leaving before another sun was set! Quickly he moved over to the broad table underneath the window, heaped with rolls and charts, one spread out flat and held at its corners with great alabaster seals, carved with the eagle of Rome. He grinned. His lord had made it easy for him.

He did not understand the names written on the land of Britain, but knew the bold label of the country.

"And only my lord," he thought, "has charted this place, so this must be her forest and her hills." He found the points of the sun, and the landing place, etched clearly with its fleet of little ships. The clear neat writing of his lord, showed where crops grew: small rings for settlements, dark shading for the rising of the hills, and neat crossed lines for water. The rising sun always to the hand that threw her spear, turning always a little away from it as she went. The long hills up from the sea she would already know, and the deep valley filled with forest. Then, on the next line of hills she should be above her lake. Madness that she should go at all, but if she were set, then she would find it. She had not been too long in Rome to forget all her forest and her lake had taught her.

He jumped at the trumpet blaring for dismiss, already in his mind traveling with the girl through the low fields from the sea, and up the green slopes of the hills, over them and through the forest, the sun always, always, he heard himself say aloud, rising to the hand that throws. Guiltily he jumped from the table, even as the crash of feet turned the soldiers toward the gates and toward the sea, toward the same forests whose paths he plotted for the girl. He did not know that Caesar, having studied all these maps, and learned his lessons from the previous summer, had decided to strike farther to the east, along the flat coastline and up the great rivers that captives told him ran into the very heart of Britain.

"But how do I get there?" she whispered urgently, when he told her how simple was the lay of the land between the landing place and the sea. "I am in Rome, and I have to get there." Irritably she looked at him, as though he could be so stupid as to forget the most important part, no use to have learned the map, if she must stay in Rome.

He made a vague dismissing gesture with his hands. They talked in desperate whispers at the door curtain of the children's room, where she watched over their sleeping through the heat of the day. The lord Durus had come home, all plans finished for Caesar and for Britain. Now he sat with Marcus and the lady Petrona in the dark vaulted steward's room, hung with keys and stacked with all the archives of the house, planning for his home while he was gone.

"We are leaving on the morning tide," he whispered.

"Who is we?"

He looked at her as if she was being simple. "The legions. You. Me."

"Me? How?" Now she looked a little frightened. Like the whole plan for the conquest of Britain, it had come too soon. A moment she glanced back into the room where the three children slept in their carved beds, soft hair clinging damply to their foreheads, and small fingers curled in sleep, as if she asked herself she could leave them. Then she turned back firmly to the boy.

"Tell me," she said.

"My lord has made it easy for us. Cassilus, he said, you will go with the wagon for my personal baggage." His teeth were white in the shadows as he grinned. "Be at the gates of the barracks by the fifteenth hour."

"Well?"

"Remember I have seen all this before. In the darkness and the uproar that is the baggage following the legions, no one will see or care whether two slaves hop onto the baggage wagons of my lord, or one. Nor see nor care whether two slaves follow it aboard."

Unbelievingly she looked at him. It could not be as simple as that. But he nodded reassuringly.

"I will give you my second tunic," he said, "when we are outside the walls." He grinned again. "It is as well we are not Romans," he said, "or I would have to cut your hair."

"They will miss me," she said, trying to foresee all the difficulties.

"Tonight the house will be at odds, because my lord is going away. Anyone who misses you will think you on an errand for someone else. Tomorrow it will be too late."

She stared at him, her eyes big, unable to believe it could be that simple, but he would not stay to reassure her more, fearful lest someone come and find them talking. He smiled at her and touched her on the arm and went away.

It was as easy as he had said. Tears threatened her at the evening meal, as she stood in her place in the shadow of the pillars and watched her young lord and his lady sitting at their flower-decked table as though this were any other night, offering serene and happy faces to their children that they might not burden them with parting, their own eyes meeting across the flowers as though they could not look enough, who might never see again. Almost she cried out to them that she was not running from them in ingratitude, that Rome had taught her gentleness and love that made her understand the grief of leaving it, where she had never known such grief before. Desperately she wanted to tell them

187

why she was going, although even in her own mind it was hardly clear enough for words. To tell my people, she said to herself, looking around at the lamplight and the flowers, the clean shining hair and happy faces of the children, the tenderness and love that lay as heavy as the perfume of the roses across the table between the young Roman and his wife. To tell my people, she whispered again, and closed her eyes against the hot misery of her tears.

As Cassilus had said, the house was at odds, the children not dismissed to bed but kept with their parents that Durus might have every precious moment of them all. Lumna found herself at the hour she had promised to meet Cassilus, adrift, exactly as he had foreseen, with none of her accustomed duties and no one to care particularly what she did. They left unnoticed by a small door in the side wall of the house, and in the tamarisk grove along the hillside, Lumna changed into the short brown tunic that made her immediately a boy.

In the crowded transport for their few days at sea, they were fortunate to have a piece of deck to sleep on, unquestioned with their bright badges on their tunics, crowded with slaves and followers of every kind. Nor did they set eyes on their master until the legions disembarked at the great camp on the southern shores of Gaul.

"Keep away from him," said Cassilus. "He is the only one to know you. Stay with his baggage wagon, and even if I do not see you, we will meet again across from Britain."

"The driver? Will he not know I do not belong to my lord?"

Cassilus looked at the tough-skinned soldier cursing his way fluently along the quay, and touched the bright badge on her tunic.

"That is all you need. Who is he to care or question how many slaves my lord brings to war. Tell him you are in charge of the baggage."

She told him nothing, because he never asked her, looking at her with the same indifference as he looked at all the crates and bundles on his wagon, marked with the house badge the same as on her tunic.

With an ease that made her hug herself with laughter, she jolted on the baggage wagon all the way up the vast land of Gaul, through the forests and the great plains split by rivers wider and grander than she had ever dreamed, seeing all the things that she had never seen on her terrible march down it in the prisoners' train, her eyes only on her own misery. She saw the townships and the thriving farms, and acres upon acres of ripening corn. Romans everywhere supervised the quarrying of stone, and the building of roads and towns, and great flying bridges that someone told her were for the carrying of water. All the things, she thought, that they will bring to Britain. She saw again the great stones marching like soldiers over the gentle hills, saw here and there the square temples of the gods, and turned her eyes away from the shriveled heads about their courts.

There was always food. The soldiers and slaves of

the baggage train were fed as well as the rest of the army, and no one questioned her. No one had time to care or think whether the slave on any baggage wagon of Durus Velanius had too soft a face for any boy, or whether he walked with a grace that he could do nothing to get rid of. Everyone was too concerned with their own business, too caught up in the driving urgency with which the baggage train thundered and jolted before the legions toward the sea.

She had the sense and patience to wait until Cassilus found her again on the north coast, where the wind blew with a remembered chill, and the shores of Britain were a blue cold line across the choppy sea.

They were careful to show no pleasure at seeing each other.

"I had forgotten it was so cold," and Cassilus looked at her pinched face and did not dare this time to offer her a share of his cloak.

"What now?" she asked, moving away a little from the driver who baked his evening bread above a small fire blue and bright with the salt flames of driftwood. "What now? Do I go charging up the beaches with the legions?"

Her long successful journey up through Gaul had given her confidence, and the grin she turned on Cassilus was almost cheeky.

He grinned back, elated too at the simplicity of their journey. "Not even I do that," he said, "and I have a right to be here."

Her smile faded. "So do I," she said, and looked at

the blue shadowy line beyond the sea. "That is my country."

He did not know what to say, still troubled and afraid at heart that she hoped for too much, that the whole idea was folly and the small words of one girl no use at all against the hostility of all the tribes. But she had her dreams, he understood, and had, it seemed, been dreaming them since long before she ever saw a Roman. They could kill her, when she went back to them with all this talk, thinking it some strange magic to destroy them.

"Lumna," he said urgently. "If—if things do not go well with your people, you will come back to the Romans, won't you?"

The old stubborn look crept back onto her face, as though to say that if she said things would go right they would go right, but the gentleness of the lady Petrona's house had taught her something, and her face relaxed.

"Of course," she said, even though secretly she did not believe it would happen.

Cassilus looked worried still. "But even if you do," he said, "you may not be able to find us. You should have something to show any Romans you find, to tell them you belong to Rome. Some Roman thing."

"I have my tattoo mark as a slave," she thought, "but it would be death to show them that."

Cassilus was feeling all over his person, seeking some small thing to give her. She put out a hand and stopped him, smiling.

"I have something," she said, and from under her tunic she pulled out the small soapstone image of Mars that he had given her a year ago, when they parted in the forest. He looked at it, his face creased in foolish delight that she should still possess it.

"You have had it all the time?" he asked incredulously, and she nodded. Then her face sobered, and she looked at the small smooth image, as though something had just struck her.

"Something brought me safely," she said, "to my lord's house."

"And will bring you there again," Cassilus said stoutly, although he was sick with fear for her that it might not. "Now I will tell you how to cross the sea."

The baggage and the slaves would go only when the legions had made a secure bridgehead and begun the establishment of a permanent camp.

"So we can go together," he said. "My lord will be with the legion, and there is no one else to care."

"And when I get there?" she asked, fearful of standing on her own land, and then having to march into some Roman camp, straight into the clear sight of her lord Durus, who would never be so vague as to be taken in by a mere boy's tunic.

Cassilus looked a little troubled. "We will have to hide you," he said, "until dark, and then slip you out between the sentries. After that, you are alone. That is the only difficult part. Roman sentries are not idle. But we will do it," he added cheerfully. "We have not come so far to be defeated by that."

Several days later, when the troop transports and the cavalry had both long disappeared into the blue distance that was Britain, they embarked in a wild welter of stores and tents and food and people, arms and ropes and carpenters' tools. All of them were accompanied by some fierce custodian determined that whatever sank to the bottom of the dark blue choppy sea, it would not be that for which he was responsible.

The thing that pleased Cassilus most was that they sailed on a late evening tide. There was no difficulty about getting aboard. It was only necessary to stand by the baggage of Durus Velanius and look fierce as though it was in their charge.

"Do you not see," he said to her, as they stood crushed between a load of horseshoes and bales of thick woolen tunics for the legionaries in the winter. "It will be dusk by the time we beach in Britain. If we are a little slow getting off our master's baggage, then you have no need at all to go inside the area of the sentries. No one will see you slip off into the dark. And the landing is at almost the same place. Your journey is exactly as the map has said."

The shingle beach when they reached it was ablaze with flares and torches, and blue-flaming piles of driftwood. Night was turned into day by the relentless Caesar, who would not waste an hour. Long before the baggage ships were dragged up the sliding beach and unloaded, thick absolute darkness held the silent land beyond the bright area of Roman light and Roman noise. Lumna looked out into it, pausing from her busy doing nothing, that had been just enough to stop anyone from noticing she was idle, and came over to where Cassilus was sorting his master's bedroll from another dozen in every way the same.

"I am going," she said, and his hands grew still on the heaped brown canvas. He did not look at her for a moment, then he straightened, and looked all around him from the frantic scene of noise and bustle out into the black night.

There was nothing he could say, although some frantic voice inside him screamed that he must not let her go, that if he did, it was her death, and he would never see her more, either here or on the sunny hill in Rome. Screamed at him to hold her and drag her to his lord, and beg him to shut her somewhere and keep her safe.

"Do not go too fast," was all he said, his voice hoarse and tight and in the bright firelight, she nodded. Then she left, quietly, so that no one even saw her go. He tried not to watch her, but could not help it, bending over his task so that people did not see his eyes fixed on the small figure growing shadowy first and then melting totally into the black darkness lying beyond the lights of safety.

Chapter Twelve

SHE kept the red morning sky as she had been told, at each sunrise, on the hand that threw her spear, turning her shoulder a little against it as she walked. In the late daylight of the third day, when a cold snake of fear had begun to twist within her mind, she came down suddenly out of the trees onto the banks of a slow, reed-grown river. A few moments she stood, with the marshy grass cold about her feet, and the shadows creeping from the trees, then she leaned against the ribbed trunk of an ancient willow, with her face against the bark, struggling with scalding tears, unfamiliar tears that of late had come so easily to her. Beyond the next ridge was her lake. She had come here often to fish, with the other young ones of the tribe, when for some poor season, the fish in the lake was not enough to feed the tribe. Blindly, almost, she had walked, guided only by the sun, turning from her way twice when worn tracks had shown her to be near some settlement. She dozed uneasily at night in trees high enough for safety from the bigger animals, and listened for them always in the day, her hand tight about her spears, and every rustle in the forest tangles a promise of her death. But something had guided her to the lake. One more night of clinging in some tree and in the morning she would cross the hill and find the paths familiar on the other side. Her hand crept unbidden to the string around her neck, and found the warm, smooth comfort of the small Roman god. The god of war, Cassilus had said. If it were he who had cared for her on this journey, it was not because she asked for war. Now that she was close, only the darkening hill between her and the faces of her people, she began to tremble a little, finding it difficult in this dusky marsh to believe at all in the sun-drenched city beyond the sea, and all the things she had learned there. How was she to tell her people? The frogs mocked her hoarsely from the edges of the river, and in the half light bats whistled past her head. The last birds twittered at her from the forest at her back, and she felt alone and hopeless, as though it were a strange land.

Relief at finding herself close to the lake was fled. Never had she known such loneliness. She stood in the cold dusk with the fires of her people burning like those of strangers beyond the hill, her fingers desperate around the figure of some Roman god. Neither of them could help her, and she could only turn as firmly as she could, back across the boggy grass into the trees, to find safety and shelter for the night.

The lake was exactly as she had left it, thin, weedy crops of grain in the few fields below the forest, and the scraggy cattle roaming to the water's edge. It was afternoon and very hot, the lake lying green and thick below its cloud of dancing flies, and the only person she passed was a man asleep in the shady edges of a thicket. At the landing place a skiff was lying, and with only one look over at the silent village beyond the causeway and the palisade, she climbed into it and broke the green stillness of the water with smooth sleek ripples that died behind her as though she had never been.

She came among them like a ghost, and they were watching her before she ever reached the causeway, nor did one of them move to speak to her or help her tie her boat. Anger was bubbling in her by the time she walked up between them and still they did not speak, only drawing back to stare at her as though she were one of the peoples of the dead. She threw her brown head into the air to stare back at them, who would give her no welcome. Then she realized where their eyes rested. She had forgotten that she was wearing still the tunic Cassilus had given her, blazoned across the breast with the house badge of the tribune, dirty and rubbed from the long, long journey, but nevertheless a bright surge of such color as they had never seen. Her anger cooled a little, and she tried desperately to remember that in the long fantastic year that had shown her so much, they had seen only the cold cycle of the winter lake, coming to the spring and summer as it had done with every year they lived.

She tried particularly hard to be calm and humble when she faced her mother, thrusting from her mind the quiet face and smooth fairness of the lady Petrona, bending her head before the squat figure with the tousled hair as formally as she had bent it in the colonnades of the villa when her lord had passed her by.

"Mother," she said, and it was as if her one word loosed something suddenly in the silent crowd that followed her, told them she was after all only Lumna the Proud, who had run away and was now come back. Their hostility was like a chariot charge, bearing down on her from all sides, until she backed against the wall of her mother's hut, holding out helpless hands to try and thrust away the crowding, shouting faces, turning from her mother to her brother and the other members of the family, as if to demand mutely what it was that she had done. It was her brother in the end, taking her father's place as chief, who held up his spear for silence and thrust his face to hers.

"You killed your father," he said bluntly. "Why do you come back here that we may kill you?"

She stared at him as if he was mad, and then even in the dreadful moment, circled by hatred and with his spear beside her throat, she almost laughed. All the long way from Rome, she had thought of nothing but the things that she would tell her people, to teach them and help them live as the Romans. And all the long winter through they had thought of nothing except that she had killed her father. She had forgotten all about it, all about the Roman spear that came in silence from the shadows of the trees, and had never thought for one moment that this was something for which she must give answer. At least it was something she could fight, instead of senseless hate without a reason.

"I did not, I did not, kill my father," she shouted at him.

"He was dead and you were gone." There was neither interest nor affection in the cold eyes that glared at her from under dark shaggy brows. She might have belonged to any tribe on earth, and not be his sister by the tie of blood.

"It was the Romans, and they took me prisoner!"

Uncomprehendingly they stared at her, as though they waited for her to say something which made sense, and in cold, sudden fear she realized that she did not have to make them believe what she had seen half across the world. She had to make them believe that the Romans even existed. Behind her on the coast they were massed to sweep across the whole land, as they had swept over Gaul, and now she understood what this would mean. But here beside the green lake where the ripples had died and the very fish slept in the failing sun, Rome and its world and its marching legions did not threaten, since they did not even exist.

Frantically she looked around for something that could show them, prove that she was speaking of real people. Her fingers found the little god about her neck, instinctively as though she sought his help, and then she turned to her brother, sharply.

"Have you the spear that killed my father?"

He had drawn it from his back himself. He nodded, unwillingly.

"Bring it! Bring it here to me!"

There was something fierce and desperate about her that made him do as she said, some authority, child though she was, that was foreign to them and to the sullen, silent Lumna they had known in the years before. He made a sign to a man behind him, who trotted to the hut that was the armory of the tribe. While he was gone they stared at her in silence, and she stared back at them as though willing them to listen to her when the moment came.

She seized the spear when it was brought, thrusting the head almost into her brother's astonished face.

"See that," she cried. "Is that the spear of our tribe?"

His face crinkled in its mat of hair, and he followed her fingers around the spearhead—its curves rounder than any forged in the village.

"Another tribe," he said indifferently, and she shouted at him then.

"Yes," she cried. "Another spear from another tribe. Then how could I use it to kill my father?" Urgently she seized his tunic, feeling the coarseness and the grease under her fingers. "It does belong to another tribe. I know it does. I saw my father killed with it!" She had to stop for the buzz of derision for such a story. "That is why I came back, to tell you of this tribe, who are very great and fierce and will wipe our people off the lake and kill them all, if you do not know of them. I have been their prisoner all the year."

There was some intensity about her that disturbed even his slow brain, and after staring at her a long time, and lifting a dirty hand to finger the bright-colored badge on her breast, he at last nodded his head slowly but disparagingly, as though she might tell, but she must not expect him to believe. He gestured her into the family hut.

At first they listened incredulously, and then after some time, first one of them laughed and then another and another, until the whole, stuffy, smoke-filled hut was a rocking mass of laughter, and that was all she got. They did not even care any more about whether or not she had killed her father. She was too simple to have done even that. Poor Lumna, touched now by the foolishness of the poor ones who could not contribute to the tribe but lived like children in their own secret worlds. One by one, they got up, still laughing, and walked out, and in the end only her mother and her brother were left, looking at her with shame that she should have made such a fool of them before the tribe.

"They are coming, I tell you," she cried helplessly. "They are coming!" Tears of misery and desperation poured down her face; of all things, she had not thought that they would laugh. "They are coming, and you will think them gods as I did." Sudden aching loneliness seized her for Cassilus, her friend, and the bright Roman garden and the small tumbling children, for the scent of roses and the kind, austere face of Durus Velanius. "And they are people," she cried in anguish. "People, like ourselves."

Suddenly the tears left her, and cold knowledge took her of the impossibility of what she had tried to do. Cassilus was right, she was a fool. And a child. What could she do. She looked from her mother to her brother and they looked back with empty eyes—without understanding.

"No," she said then, "not like ourselves. But they are people."

After that they ignored her, more contemptuous of her than they had ever been, her progress around the village followed by snickers they did not even try to hide. In her own family hut, it was as though she had never been away, submerged again in all ugly tasks at the lakeside home, all the dirt and squalor and ill temper that she had been so happy to forget. The only difference was the almost fearful slantwise glances her mother was always casting at her, even while she drove her with all her old ferocity. In the darkness and the smoke and the noise of howling babies and all the ugliness that had become like a troubled dream, Lumna fought to hold to the reality of her far off Roman spring, and the need to stay with her tribe, to be with them when the Romans came, that she might help them to understand each other. They *would* come, and then her tribe would believe her, and listen to her, if only she were fast enough, and they not all killed first. Occasionally still she would try to make her brother listen, until he turned on her one day, his hairy face no more than an inch from her own.

"The place for the simple," he breathed at her menacingly, "is at the bottom of the lake. There I will put you if you trouble me more with your fancies."

She knew he meant it, and from that day onward, did not speak of the Romans again. But she watched her tribe as she might watch those about to die, fingering the small god at her throat and wondering if she would get any chance to show it, before she was killed with all the rest.

Whenever she could slip away from them, she climbed up the familiar path to the place of the Ancient People, passing the spot where her father was killed, and seeing them all as clearly as if they stood in reality around her in the dappled shadows. But there was no flashing light on the hills in the distance, and when she rolled back the stone and walked down the long, cool passage, the great chamber was empty, the ceiling silent in her silence, and no mark of footprints save her own.

Within a while she had begun to wonder if the impossible had happened, and conquering Rome had been defeated down there by the sea, beaten back to Gaul by the naked tribesmen, never to come again, leaving her here forever in a wattle hut, the simpleton of her tribe.

The sun was blazing through the rich days of the year and the thin corn ripening in the fields about the lake, when she saw a man come running from the forest, and pole himself madly across the lake, to charge through the village scattering the people and shouting for her brother. When he came on her, he stopped a moment in his rush, to stare at her with an expression of astonishment and fear, and then her brother rushed at him, hearing the shouting. There was urgency and fright in every gesture. The man pointed over toward the sunrise where the ground dropped at the end of a long ridge of hills which fell at its near end down to the lake. Words poured from him, but Lumna, some fierce excited sense telling her what he had seen, could not hear him, could only cling to her small war god and try to still her thudding heart, holding up her head and catching firmly the glances shot at her by her brother. She saw the man shaking his head as though denying something vigorously, and her brother staring at her then.

They had come.

No word was said to her through all the horn blowing, summoning the men from the fields, and the long haranguing of them by her brother. Nor, through the gathering of their spears and shields and slings, and their mustering boatload by boatload in the fields on the lake shore, excited, barely knowing what they were about. They had never fought before, and only understood that when he gave the word, they were to kill, as they would kill the wild boar on a forest hunt, for if they did not, they would be killed themselves.

Only when they had drifted off into the forest, as silent in it as if they tracked the wild boar in truth, did her brother come and seize her by the tunic neck, with him a few more of the head men of the village who had listened to her wild stories of the Romans.

"They have come," she said to him triumphantly, even though his hand bruised her neck to agony, and he looked at her as if he could gladly kill her for being right.

"You will tell us what they are," he said.

"People," she said desperately. "Only people, and many of them speak a tongue like ours and you could talk to them."

He did not even trouble to answer such foolishness and thrust her on before him at his spear tip toward the forest, watched in silence now and fear by the women, crowding at their huts, who had gathered wild stories from the departing men about great metal monsters in the forest, brought there by the girl.

The sun had slanted a good section of the sky as they walked along the high, wooded ridge, before the first scouts of their people came slipping to them out of the trees, soundless as the birds flying in their branches, whispering in low excited voices to her brother. He nodded and then grasped the girl, and she felt the tip of his knife prick against her ribs.

"They are here," he whispered to her, "whatever they may be. On the far slope of the hill. They are surrounded by the tribe, but our people are fearful. You will come, silently you will come, and look at these creatures and tell us what they are that we may destroy them."

Hopelessly she looked at them.

"People," she said. "They are but people."

The knife pricked her ribs and she moved on, more silent even than the rest, lest by some noise she frighten the already terrified tribe into starting to kill. Even now she hoped to stop them.

When they stopped, she could sense, if not see, the tribe all around her in the forest, even as they had surrounded her in the wood above the cornfields, ready to plunge down from their silence with howling war cries and surprising death.

Carefully she thrust aside the leaves and looked down through the scattered bushes on the slope of the hill. They had set their sentries with all their usual care, but the woodcraft of the Britons had defeated them, so that Lumna looked down almost into the eyes of a Roman, alert and watchful under his headpiece, but unaware that the green thickets at which he stared were already bristling with spears and ablaze with hostile eyes.

Caesar had decided to strike father east from the landing place. The corn and water had not been mapped, and scouts must go ahead again. It was almost without surprise that Lumna saw them farther down the hill, Durus Velanius sitting on the sloping grass with his tablets on his knees, his smooth head bent above them; she could sense his long fingers moving on the surface of the wax. Over to the right, she could see in the thickets the movement and bustle of the men pitching their small camp for the night, and even as she watched,

Flavius the centurion moved out from among them and came over to his officer, square head bare to the heat, steady and competent eyes flicking over everything. Almost she smiled a moment, in pure affection for the broad, good-natured face, and then she saw Cassilus, drifting around the edge of the ring, inside the sentries, picking up wood for his fire.

Even then, her only fear was for her own people, who should be allowed to live, and to live as Romans did, and not in their wattle huts and smoke and dirt. These people down the hill with the sun sparking a hundred lights from the moving metal of their clothes were her friends, who would help her, if she could only reach them before they were angered by some careless spear thrown by a tribesman who did not understand. Then all her people would be killed, and other tribes and others, and never know what she had known.

"Cassilus," she whispered, and looked in anguish from her brother to the man on her other side. The men all around her were simmering with impatience, their eyes wild with a lust for battle they had never known, only understanding that these creatures down the hill offered more excitement than any boar to hunt. But they were disciplined to the chase, and held their hands, crouched to act on the instant of a signal. "Cassilus."

"What are they?" her brother whispered, and even in his eyes there was a thread of fear of the bright metal in the sun, and the strange close-fitting clothes of the moving men. "What are they?"

"*People*," Lumna hissed in exasperation. "Romans. They are warriors, and will kill you. Talk to them I *beg* you."

Cassilus was coming close now, unarmed, singing a little, his arms full of gathered faggots, secure in the sentry ring about the camp site. Secure in his faith in the Romans, in the legions.

"See," she whispered urgently and desperately, held only from shouting at him by the firm pressure of the knife point in her side. "See, he is only a *person*. Like yourself."

It was too much for the man on the other side of her, not strictly one of the tribe, who had wandered in adrift many seasons back, and settled, taking himself a wife, and becoming one of the dwellers of the lake. He in his youth had known battle, and the fighting of the tribes. He knew what a spear was for, and could wait no longer on this talking.

Suddenly he laughed hoarsely, and she caught the wild gleam of his eye through his bush of hair, but the flight of his spear was too fast for her to follow. Almost as he laughed, it was sticking suddenly in Cassilus' throat, blood spouting dark over his brown tunic as he sank to the ground, the faggots tumbling foolishly from his arms.

"See," bellowed the man, "he dies like a person!" Lumna saw as in a dream the sentries hurl themselves back to the center of the open space, to make a shield ring with all the others, exactly as in the cornfield. She felt rather than saw the man reach across her and snatch the horn from her brother's hand, sounding the signal for the hunt, and the tribe knew the sight of blood as well as he did. Fear vanished and war cries screamed out that they never knew they knew; the flight of spears was faster than the running soldiers. She heard the man howl with laughter as he leapt over her.

"People," he bellowed. "People!" and her brother echoed his laughter as he launched a spear past his racing head.

She did not look after she saw Durus go down, his dark head split; wrenched with her own horror and with it in the instant the horror of the loneliness and grief that would fall like the evening shadows over the white villa on the hill.

A moment she paused, staring as though halted by the terror of all the sorrow there was to come. Then she fished frantically for her small war god, and began to run, holding him in her hand and weeping as she ran. It was almost dark before she thought to look at the blood-red setting sun, and be sure that she was heading for the sea.

MADELEINE POLLAND planned to be a painter after completing school in England, but circumstances changed her decision. During World War II she served for four years with the W.A.A.F. and it was then that she first began to write—short plays and entertainments for her friends. After the war she was married, and a home and two children kept her occupied until 1960, when a friend suggested that she write a book. She did just that, and *Children of the Red King* was selected as an Honor Book in the New York *Herald Tribune* Spring Book Festival. Since then she has written many books for young readers: *Beorn the Proud*, also a *Herald Tribune* Honor Book, *The Town Across the Water*, *The Queen's Blessing*, *The White Twilight*, *Queen Without Crown*, and *To Tell My People*. Mrs. Polland and her family live in the country outside of London.

A dedicated interest in history has made the settings of Mrs. Polland's books authentic. Of *To Tell My People* Mrs. Polland says that the book had its origin in a sense of atmosphere evoked in her by the locality in which the story takes place. While visiting in that district she describes, ". . . suddenly feeling how it must have been to the ancient people who watched the far hills for an enemy coming over them from the sea."

RICHARD M. POWERS was born in Chicago and studied at the Art Institute of Chicago, the University of Illinois, and the New School for Social Research. The father of four children, he lives in Ridgefield, Connecticut, where he enjoys landscape gardening and tennis as well as writing and painting. Mr. Powers is a noted illustrator of magazines and books and his work has been shown in the Society of Illustrators' exhibits. Also a painter, his paintings have been included in various major exhibits at the Museum of Modern Art, the Corcoran Biennial, and the National Academy, among others.

ABOUT THE BOOK: Caslon Antique was used for display and initial letters; the text was set in linotype Janson. The book was printed by offset. Illustrator Richard M. Powers customarily uses a technique that is closely equivalent to his text. He observed, "In *To Tell My People*, I have tried to emphasize the brooding, ominous quality of the story-line which relates the struggles of a semi-savage Celtic girl caught between two warring cultures—the dead-end savage culture of the ancient Britons and the sophisticated juggernaut culture of the Romans. For this reason I have employed devices calculated to impart a sense of tension, conflict, even the state of mind of the girl—heavy black areas, brutal textures, and a wild, warlike line. If I have succeeded, these devices should give strong amplification to the text."